The Sunset Park Chronicles
A Journey of Laughter, Friendship, and Endless Memories
By Kevin James Joseph McNamara

Published By Kevin James Joseph McNamara

As always, the advice of a competent professional should be sought. The author and publisher do not warrant the performance, effectiveness or applicability of any sites listed or linked to in this eBook. All links are for information purposes only and are not warranted for content, accuracy or any other implied or explicit purpose.

Table Of Contents:

Prologue

~ ~ ~

~ ~ ~

Epilogue

~ ~ ~

Dedication

~ ~ ~ ~ ~

Prologue

In the heart of Brooklyn, nestled between the bustling streets and the quiet waters of the bay, lies a neighborhood that has seen it all. Sunset Park, a place where cultures melded, dreams were forged, and lifelong friendships were woven into the very fabric of the community.

Our story begins not with grand heroes or epic adventures, but with a group of eight friends who, over the years, discovered that the ordinary moments of life could be extraordinary when shared with those who utterly understood them. These friends came from diverse backgrounds, each bringing a unique perspective, and their bonds were forged through laughter, support, and a profound sense of unity.

As we journey through the pages of "The Sunset Park Chronicles," we will witness the laughter that echoed through the streets, the tears that watered the dreams, and the enduring spirit that defined this remarkable group. Their stories, filled with humor, diversity, and unwavering friendship, serve as a testament to the enduring power of human connection.

Join us as we embark on a heartwarming journey through the decades, a tale of love, loss, hope, and resilience. Through every twist and turn, these friends for life remind us that even in the most ordinary of places, extraordinary stories are waiting to be told.

~ ~ ~ ~ ~

1. "The First Day"

The kindergarten classroom in Sunset Park, Brooklyn, was buzzing with excitement on that fateful first day. Eight diverse children, each with a unique background and personality, walked into the room, completely unaware of the lifelong bonds they were about to forge.

Ms. Martinez, their kindergarten teacher, welcomed them with a warm smile. "Good morning, children! Today, we have a special treat. We're going to play a game so we can all get to know each other better."

Little did she know that her plan for a simple icebreaker would turn into a comedy of errors and the birth of a lifelong friendship.

As the children gathered in a circle, they introduced themselves one by one.

"Hi, I'm Alex," said a dark-haired boy with a mischievous glint in his eye. "I'm Greek, and I'm here to report that I've already uncovered a conspiracy involving missing crayons."

Laughter rippled through the group as they exchanged amused glances. Alex's dry, witty humor was apparent right from the start.

Lei, a quiet Chinese-American girl with glasses, followed. "I'm Lei. I like computers more than people, and my favorite color is hexadecimal code #42A4D8."

There was a brief pause as the other kids tried to process Lei's unexpected humor, but soon they were all chuckling.

Rashida, a vivacious African-American girl, introduced herself next. "I'm Rashida, and I'm going to be a famous actress someday! Just you wait!" She then did an impromptu cartwheel, which ended in a comical fall that had everyone in stitches.

Carlos, a Puerto Rican boy with a perpetual smile, said, "I'm Carlos, and I'm going to be a famous musician! And if that doesn't work out, I'll be a professional bubblegum bubble blower."

The kids erupted in laughter at Carlos's infectious optimism.

Fatima, a Pakistani-American girl with a serious expression, introduced herself with a hint of sarcasm. "I'm Fatima. My parents want me to be a doctor, but I secretly dream of being a circus performer."

Elena, a sharp-tongued Russian-Jewish girl, followed with a smirk. "I'm Elena, and I already have a law degree. Do not mess with me!"

Sean, an Irish-American boy with bright red hair, chimed in, "I'm Sean, and I'm training to be a firefighter. So, if things get too hot in here, just call me."

Maya, a lively Afro-Latina girl, completed the introductions with a flourish. "I'm Maya, and I'm an artist. My favorite thing in the world is painting, especially when I am covered head to toe in colorful splatters!"

Ms. Martinez could not help but chuckle at the group's diverse and spirited introductions. "Well, it seems like we have quite the bunch of characters here. Let us play a game of 'Two Truths and a Lie' to get to know each other even better."

The children eagerly took turns sharing funny, imaginative "truths" and "lies" about themselves. Alex claimed he had once interviewed a talking parrot for a newspaper, Lei said she could communicate with her computer using interpretive dance, Rashida claimed she could juggle invisible oranges, and Carlos insisted he once sang a duet with a subway rat.

As the game continued, the laughter grew louder, and the initial awkwardness of meeting new people faded away. It was clear that these eight kindergarteners had a natural chemistry, fueled by their humor and diversity.

As the day went on, they shared crayons, traded jokes, and even collaborated on a crayon-based conspiracy theory that left everyone in stitches. By the end of that first day, they were not just classmates but fast friends, united by their shared love of laughter and their ability to find humor in the quirks of life.

And so, their journey as "friends for life" began, with a camaraderie built on witty banter, humorous misunderstandings, and the promise of countless adventures ahead in the culturally rich and ever-evolving landscape of Sunset Park, Brooklyn. Little did they know that their laughter would echo through the decades, creating a lifetime of cherished memories and unbreakable bonds.

2. "Lost and Found."

Two years had passed since their first day in kindergarten, and the group of eight friends had grown even closer. They were now in second grade, and a new school year brought new adventures.

Their teacher, Mrs. Johnson, was a kind and patient woman who admired the diversity of her students. She encouraged them to embrace their individuality and celebrate their unique backgrounds.

One sunny September morning, as the children gathered in their classroom, a sense of excitement filled the air. It was show-and-tell day, and they could not wait to share their treasures with one another.

"Alright, class," Mrs. Johnson announced with a smile, "who would like to go first for show-and-tell today?"

Alex, never one to shy away from the spotlight, eagerly raised his hand. "I've got something special to share, Mrs. Johnson."

With a twinkle in his eye, Alex reached into his backpack and pulled out a rubber chicken, which he proudly placed on his desk.

"This," he declared, "is Mr. Chuckles, the world's funniest rubber chicken. He has been my loyal companion for years."

Lei, with her dry sense of humor, raised an eyebrow and deadpanned, "I didn't know rubber chickens could be funny."

Alex grinned. "Oh, you would be surprised, Lei. Just wait until you hear his stand-up routine."

The classroom erupted in laughter as Alex began to mimic Mr. Chuckles' comical "bawk-bawk" noises, and even the usually reserved Lei could not help but chuckle.

Rashida was next, and she brought along a whoopee cushion, much to everyone's delight. She demonstrated its use with a dramatic flair, causing gales of laughter to fill the room.

Carlos, always the optimist, proudly presented his favorite kazoo, proclaiming that it had the power to turn any frown upside down. He then played a cheerful tune that had the whole class humming along.

Fatima, the aspiring doctor, showed off a miniature skeleton model. "This is Mr. Bones," she said, "and he's my study buddy for anatomy lessons."

Elena, ever the lawyer in training, presented a gavel and declared, "I hereby call this class to order! Let the silliness commence!"

Sean, the firefighter, shared a toy firetruck and demonstrated how it could spray imaginary water. "Never too early to learn fire safety!" he quipped.

Maya, the artist, unveiled a colorful abstract painting that she had created. "This painting represents the beauty of our diversity," she explained. "It's a celebration of all the colors that make us unique."

As the show-and-tell continued, the children marveled at each other's unique treasures and talents. The diversity of their backgrounds and interests had always been a source of wonder and amusement for them.

However, the highlight of the day came when Maya realized that her beloved paintbrush, a cherished gift from her grandmother, was missing. She frantically searched her backpack and desk, but it was nowhere to be found.

Tears welled up in Maya's eyes as she explained the situation to her friends. "I cannot find my paintbrush anywhere! It is really special to me, and I do not know what to do."

The group immediately sprang into action, determined to help their dear friend. They turned the classroom upside down, searching high and low for the missing paintbrush. They checked under desks, inside cubbies, and even in Mr. Chuckles' rubber chicken feathers.

Despite their best efforts, the paintbrush remained elusive. Carlos, ever the optimist, tried to cheer Maya up. "Do not worry, Maya. We will find your paintbrush, even if we have to organize a search party!"

Fatima, with her practicality, suggested, "Maybe we should ask Mrs. Johnson if anyone borrowed it by mistake."

Elena, always quick with her wit, added, "Or maybe Mr. Chuckles is pulling a prank and hiding it."

The group chuckled at the thought, but their determination remained strong. They knew that Maya's paintbrush was more than just a tool; it was a piece of her identity and a source of inspiration for her artwork.

With their combined efforts and humor, they eventually found the missing paintbrush tucked away in a corner of the art supply cabinet. It had rolled there during cleanup the previous day.

Maya's eyes sparkled with gratitude as she held her paintbrush tightly. "Thank you, my wonderful friends. You always know how to turn any situation into an adventure."

Their laughter echoed through" the classroom once again, and as they continued with show-and-tell, they could not help but marvel at the bond they had forged. It was a bond built on diversity, humor, and a willingness to stand by each other through thick and thin.

As they looked around at their classmates, they realized that their friendship was a shining example of how different backgrounds and unique talents could come together to create something truly magical. And so, their second-grade adventure had strengthened their bond even further, leaving them eager to see what the future had in store for their "friends for life."

3. "Cultural Collage"

Two more years had passed, and the group of eight friends, now nine years old, found themselves in the midst of a new adventure. Their teacher, Mr. Rodriguez, was known for his passion for exploring different cultures and traditions, and he had a special assignment for his class.

"Good morning, class," Mr. Rodriguez announced with enthusiasm. "Today, we are going on a journey of cultural exploration right here in Sunset Park. Each of you will share a family tradition that represents your heritage, highlighting the rich diversity of our neighborhood."

The students were excited about the prospect of learning about each other's backgrounds and traditions. They knew that their friendship was like a tapestry, woven together with threads of humor and diversity, and they were eager to see how each tradition would add to the colorful fabric.

Alex, with his Greek heritage, went first. He explained, "In my family, we have a tradition called 'The Great Olive Challenge.' Every year, we gather to see who can eat the most olives without making a funny face."

Lei, always full of unexpected humor, quipped, "Do you win by making the least funny face?"

The class erupted in laughter, and Alex grinned. "Well, sometimes it's not about winning; it's about enjoying the delicious chaos."

Rashida, the aspiring actor, shared her family tradition next. "In my house, we have 'Comedy Night.' We take turns performing the silliest, most over-the-top skits we can produce. It is all about making each other laugh."

Carlos, with his Puerto Rican roots, explained, "In Puerto Rico, we celebrate 'Three Kings' Day' with a big parade. I once thought I could be one of the kings, but I ended up tripping over my own feet during the audition."

Fatima, the future doctor, shared her family's tradition of making homemade samosas together. "It is a labor of love, and we take turns folding the perfect triangle. Sometimes, they come out looking more like abstract art than samosas!"

Elena, with her sharp wit, added, "I'm sure your samosas taste better than they look."

Sean, the Irish-American peacemaker, spoke up. "In my family, we have 'St. Patrick's Day Treasure Hunts.' We hide pots of gold (chocolate ones) all over the house, and the person who finds the most pots gets bragging rights for the year."

Maya, the artist, shared her tradition of creating vibrant carnival masks with her family during the annual Afro-Latino Carnival in Brooklyn. "It's a way to celebrate our Afro-Latina heritage and embrace our identity."

Lei, with her dry humor, teased, "Do you ever accidentally paint your own face instead of the mask?"

Maya laughed. "Well, there have been a few colorful mishaps along the way."

As the students continued to share their family traditions, the classroom transformed into a cultural kaleidoscope. They learned about Greek dance nights, Chinese lantern festivals, African-American storytelling gatherings, Puerto Rican music jam sessions, Pakistani feasts, Russian-Jewish Hanukkah celebrations, and Irish step dance-offs.

Throughout the presentations, the group could not help but add their own humor to the mix. They cracked jokes, exchanged playful banter, and even reenacted some of the traditions in a comical way. Each tradition became a piece of the puzzle, fitting perfectly into their diverse and harmonious friendship.

Mr. Rodriguez was impressed not only by the students' willingness to embrace and celebrate each other's cultures but also by the humor they infused into the presentations. He knew that their friendship was a shining example of how humor and diversity could create a beautiful mosaic of connections.

As the day came to an end, the students left the classroom with a deeper understanding of each other's backgrounds and a stronger bond than ever. Their laughter and curiosity had once again led them on an adventure of exploration, this time into the colorful tapestry of their cultural heritage.

And as they walked through the vibrant streets of Sunset Park, they could not help but appreciate the rich diversity that surrounded them, knowing that their friendship was a testament to the beauty and strength of their neighborhood's cultural collage. They were ready for whatever adventures lay ahead, united by their shared laughter and the deep respect they held for each other's traditions.

The following week, as the students continued to delve into their cultural explorations, they decided to take their learning beyond the classroom. They planned a weekend excursion to explore Sunset Park's cultural diversity firsthand.

Their adventure began at the local Sunset Park Farmers' Market, where they discovered a world of flavors and ingredients from various cultures. Maya, with her artistic eye, marveled at the vibrant array of fruits and vegetables, while Rashida could not resist mimicking the lively banter of the market vendors with her slapstick humor.

Carlos, always the optimist, sampled every type of food available, declaring each one the best he had ever tasted. His exaggerated reactions and comical food critiques had his friends in stitches.

Next, they visited the Sunset Park Library, where they explored books from different countries and cultures. Alex could not resist making puns about every title he came across, leaving the group in fits of laughter.

At a nearby park, they stumbled upon a group of people practicing traditional Chinese martial arts. Lei, with her interest in technology, recorded their graceful movements on her smartphone. She then added her own dry commentary, turning the serene practice into a hilarious video that they watched on the spot.

Their cultural journey continued as they visited a local mosque, a Russian Orthodox church, and a Chinese temple. Each visit gave them a glimpse into the religious and spiritual practices of their neighbors, and they embraced the opportunity to ask questions and learn from each other.

The day concluded with a visit to a Puerto Rican community center, where they joined in a lively salsa dance class. Carlos, in his typically enthusiastic fashion, twirled and spun his friends around the dance floor, resulting in an impromptu dance-off that had everyone laughing and clapping along.

As they headed home, exhausted but happy, they could not help but reflect on the incredible adventure they had shared. Their exploration of Sunset Park's diversity had not only deepened their understanding of different cultures but had also strengthened their bond as friends.

Back in their classroom, they eagerly shared their experiences with Mr. Rodriguez, who was delighted by their enthusiasm for learning and their ability to find humor in every situation.

"Class," he said with a smile, "you have shown that laughter and curiosity are the keys to understanding and embracing our diverse world. Your friendship is a shining example of how humor and diversity can come together to create something uniquely beautiful."

And so, their adventure of cultural exploration became a cherished memory, a reminder that their friendship was a tapestry woven with threads of humor, diversity, and a shared sense of wonder. As they looked ahead to the future, they knew that their bond would only grow stronger with each new adventure, united by their laughter and their deep appreciation for the rich mosaic of cultures that surrounded them in Sunset Park, Brooklyn.

THE GREAT SCHOOL PLAY

4. "The Great School Play"

Two more years had passed, and the group of eight friends, now eleven years old, found themselves facing a new adventure that would test their bonds in unexpected ways. Their new teacher, Mrs. Anderson, had decided that their class would put on a school play to highlight their talents and celebrate the diverse backgrounds of Sunset Park.

The play was an ambitious production that incorporated elements from different cultures, reflecting the multicultural tapestry of their neighborhood. Each member of the group had a role to play, and they were determined to make it a success.

As the rehearsals began, it became clear that their diversity, humor, and friendship dynamics would play a significant role in shaping the outcome of the play.

Alex, always the quick wit, was cast as the lead character, a journalist on a quest for truth and justice. He could not resist injecting political satire into his lines, causing the cast and crew to burst into laughter during rehearsals.

Lei, with her dry and unexpected humor, played the role of a mysterious tech genius who provided crucial information to Alex's character. Her deadpan delivery had everyone in stitches, and even the director could not help but crack a smile.

Rashida, the aspiring actor known for her slapstick comedy, was cast as a bumbling detective who stumbled through scenes with comedic grace. Her physical humor had the audience rolling with laughter during every run-through.

Carlos, the ever-optimistic Puerto Rican musician, played a musician searching for his lost muse. His heartfelt, albeit comically naive, attempts to find inspiration had the entire cast in fits of giggles.

Fatima, the Pakistani-American future doctor, portrayed a wise and nurturing elder who offered guidance to the other characters. Her attempts to speak in proverbs often led to hilarious misunderstandings.

Elena, with her sharp tongue and heart of gold, took on the role of a no-nonsense lawyer who provided legal counsel to the characters. Her deadpan humor and witty one-liners added a layer of complexity to her character.

Sean, the Irish-American peacemaker, played the role of a firefighter who came to the rescue in times of crisis. His exaggerated rescues and unintentional mishaps had the audience roaring with laughter.

Maya, the Afro-Latina artist, portrayed a painter who used her art to explore her identity. Her character's eccentricities and colorful dialogues made for some of the play's most memorable moments.

As the days passed, the group's rehearsals were marked by comical mishaps and unexpected surprises. There were moments when lines were forgotten, props were misplaced, and scenes dissolved into uncontrollable laughter.

One memorable incident occurred when Carlos, in an attempt to play a musical interlude, accidentally dropped his guitar, causing it to emit a loud, off-key chord that sent the cast and crew into hysterics. Rashida, true to her slapstick style, even incorporated the mishap into her character's comedic routine.

Another time, during a dramatic courtroom scene featuring Elena's character, a stuffed parrot (a nod to Alex's Greek heritage) was supposed to serve as evidence. However, the parrot mysteriously disappeared backstage, leading to a comical search that culminated in its triumphant return.

Through it all, the group's friendship dynamics remained strong. They supported each other during the challenging moments, and their ability to find humor in every situation brought them closer together. Mrs. Anderson, their patient and understanding teacher, could not help but admire their camaraderie and resilience.

As the day of the school play approached, the excitement and nervousness grew. The group knew that their performance would be a reflection of their friendship, humor, and diverse backgrounds. They were determined to make it a memorable and entertaining show for their classmates, families, and the entire Sunset Park community.

The night of the performance arrived, and the auditorium was filled with eager faces. As the curtains rose, the group stepped onto the stage, ready to bring their unique blend of humor and diversity to life.

The play unfolded with laughter and applause from the audience. Alex's witty one-liners, Lei's unexpected humor, Rashida's slapstick antics, Carlos's optimism, Fatima's wise proverbs, Elena's sharp retorts, Sean's heroic rescues, and Maya's colorful dialogues all came together to create a memorable performance.

Despite the comical mishaps and unexpected surprises, the group's bond shone through, and their audience could not help but be enchanted by their friendship dynamics and the rich tapestry of cultures that they represented.

As the final curtain fell, the auditorium erupted in applause and cheers. The group took their well-deserved bows, their laughter echoing through the space. Their performance was not just a testament to their talent but also a celebration of their enduring friendship and the beauty of their diversity.

Backstage, they gathered for a group hug, their hearts full of pride and gratitude. They knew that their journey together was far from over, and that whatever adventures lay ahead, they would face them with humor, diversity, and the unbreakable bonds of friendship that had been their guiding light from the very beginning.

The following weeks were a whirlwind of celebrations and compliments. Their fellow students praised their performance, and their families could not have been prouder. They received heartfelt letters from members of the Sunset Park community, expressing gratitude for highlighting the neighborhood's diversity and humor.

But as the excitement settled, the group found themselves reflecting on the journey they had taken together. They realized that the play had not just been about entertaining others; it had been an opportunity for them to grow and evolve as individuals and as friends.

Alex, who had always been quick with a joke, discovered the power of satire in addressing real-world issues. He began to write articles for the school newspaper, using humor to shed light on important topics.

Lei, whose dry humor had charmed everyone, started a tech club at school, where she shared her passion for technology with her classmates, adding a touch of unexpected humor to her presentations.

Rashida, the queen of slapstick comedy, began volunteering at a local children's hospital, using her humor to bring smiles to the faces of young patients and their families.

Carlos, whose optimism had always been infectious, continued to pursue his music dreams, even in the face of challenges. His determination inspired those around him.

Fatima, with her wisdom and nurturing spirit, found herself drawn to volunteering at a community center, where she mentored younger children, sharing her insights and proverbs with them.

Elena, whose sharp wit had made her a standout, used her legal knowledge to advocate for social justice causes, proving that humor and intelligence could be a powerful combination.

Sean, the peacemaker of the group, continued his work as a firefighter, earning the respect and admiration of his colleagues for his calm and level-headed approach to crises.

Maya explored her identity through her art even further, creating pieces that celebrated the rich cultural tapestry of Sunset Park.

Their individual journeys led to personal growth, but their friendship remained the bedrock of their lives. They continued to find joy in their shared humor, celebrate each other's successes, and support one another through challenges.

As they entered their teenage years, they faced new adventures and complexities. Crushes, school dances, and the challenges of adolescence brought both laughter and tears, but they navigated it all together.

Their friendship continued to grow in complexity, just as they did individually.

Sunset Park remained their anchor, a place where they could always return to the warmth of their friendship and the beauty of their diverse community. The years passed, and their bond only deepened, proving that through humor, diversity, and the enduring strength of friendship, they could face any challenge life threw their way.

And so, the group of eight friends, whose journey had begun in kindergarten, looked ahead to the future with anticipation and excitement. They knew that whatever adventures lay ahead, they would face them together, armed with their unique blend of humor, diversity, and the unbreakable bonds of friendship that had been their greatest treasure since that first day in Sunset Park, Brooklyn.

5. "Summer of Surprises"

Two more years had come and gone, and the group of eight friends, now thirteen years old, found themselves on the cusp of their teenage years. The summer had arrived, bringing with it the promise of adventure and new experiences in their beloved Sunset Park.

Their school days had ended, and the transition to a new chapter in their lives was approaching. With each passing year, they had grown in complexity, navigating the ups and downs of adolescence while holding onto the humor and diversity that had always defined their friendship.

As the summer sunbathed Sunset Park in warmth, the group decided to make the most of their break by embarking on a series of neighborhood explorations and fun-filled escapades.

Their adventures began with a visit to Sunset Park's famous Greenmarket, where they marveled at the colorful array of fresh fruits, vegetables, and artisanal products. Maya, with her artist's eye, could not resist sketching the vibrant scene, capturing the essence of the market's diversity in her notebook.

Alex, always quick with a quip, approached a fruit stand and joked, "Do these apples come with a side of political commentary?"

The vendor laughed and replied, "Only if you want them to!"

The group's laughter echoed through the market, drawing smiles from both vendors and fellow shoppers. They had a knack for finding humor in the everyday, and it was a gift they cherished.

Their explorations took them to the Sunset Park Library, where they discovered a treasure trove of books from around the world. Lei, with her love for technology, was drawn to the library's digital resources, and she could not resist sharing fascinating tech facts with her friends.

Rashida, always the performer, pretended to be a character from one of the novels and dramatically acted out a scene, earning applause and laughter from those nearby.

Carlos, in his eternal optimism, declared, "I've found the perfect book that will inspire my music career!" He held up a biography of a famous musician, his enthusiasm infectious.

Fatima, with her wisdom, explored the library's collection of medical books, a reminder of her dreams of becoming a doctor. She was already well-versed in anatomy, thanks to her family's medical discussions.

Elena, ever the sharp-witted lawyer, examined legal texts with a critical eye. She could not resist making humorous remarks about some of the more convoluted legal jargon.

Sean, the peacemaker, discovered a section on firefighting techniques and could not help but share anecdotes from his training, much to the amusement of his friends.

Their library visit ended with a group photo, capturing the diversity of their interests and the laughter that bound them together.

The summer also brought them to Sunset Park's cultural festivals. They attended the Chinese New Year celebration, danced to salsa music at the Puerto Rican Day Parade, and sampled delicious Pakistani dishes at a food festival. Each festival was a vibrant tapestry of colors, sounds, and flavors that reflected the neighborhood's rich diversity.

During the festivals, they could not resist participating in the cultural dances, even if their moves were a comical mix of enthusiasm and clumsiness. Carlos's salsa spins had his friends in stitches, and Alex, with his two left feet, managed to create a dance style all his own.

One evening, as they sat on a park bench overlooking the Manhattan skyline, the group reflected on the years that had passed and the changes that lay ahead.

"I can't believe we're almost teenagers," Rashida mused, her vibrant personality shining through even in moments of reflection.

Carlos added, "But no matter how old we get, we'll always have each other's backs."

Fatima nodded, balancing the expectations of her family with her own dreams. "And we'll continue to support each other's dreams, no matter where they lead."

Elena, with her sharp wit, quipped, "And we'll never stop finding humor in the world around us. It's what makes us who we are."

Their summer of surprises continued with a visit to a local art gallery, where they admired Maya's artwork on display. Maya had been exploring her Afro-Latina identity through her art, and her pieces had garnered attention and praise.

Lei, with her tech expertise, suggested they create a digital gallery of Maya's work to reach a wider audience. They spent hours working on the project, Lei providing the tech knowledge while Maya added her artistic touch.

As they worked together, their bond grew stronger, a testament to their ability to combine their diverse talents for a common goal.

One warm summer evening, they decided to organize a neighborhood talent show in Sunset Park. They invited friends and families, and even some local businesses sponsored the event.

Alex, with his gift for political satire, served as the host, providing witty commentary between acts. His humor set the tone for an evening of laughter and entertainment.

Lei, despite her social struggles, bravely took the stage to highlight her tech skills, demonstrating a series of innovative gadgets that left the audience in awe. Her dry humor added a unique charm to her presentation.

Rashida performed a hilarious one-woman skit that had everyone in stitches. Her slapstick comedy skills were on full display, and the crowd could not get enough.

Carlos, always optimistic, sang a heartfelt song about the power of friendship, bringing tears to the eyes of many in the audience. His music touched hearts and reminded everyone of the strength of their bonds.

Fatima, with her wisdom, shared a spoken word piece about the importance of embracing diversity and unity. Her words resonated deeply with the crowd, sparking a sense of unity, and understanding.

Elena, the sharp-tongued lawyer, delivered a passionate speech about the value of laughter and diversity in a changing world. Her words served as a reminder of the group's enduring friendship.

Sean demonstrated his firefighting skills with a dramatic rescue act that left the audience in awe. His bravery and dedication to his community were evident in every move.

Maya presented a live painting performance, creating a beautiful mural that celebrated the cultural tapestry of Sunset Park. Her art spoke volumes about the beauty of diversity.

The talent show was a resounding success, a testament to the group's ability to bring joy and laughter to their community through their unique talents. As they took their final bows, the audience erupted in applause, and the group could not help but feel a sense of pride and accomplishment.

As the summer of surprises drew to a close, the group of eight friends knew that they were entering a new phase of their lives. Their coming-of-age journey had been marked by humor, diversity, and the enduring strength of their friendship.

They had faced challenges and changes, but their bond had only grown stronger. They had celebrated each other's talents, supported each other's dreams, and found humor in every moment, no matter how complex or emotional.

As they looked ahead to the future, they were filled with anticipation and curiosity about what lay ahead. But one thing was certain: they would face it together, armed with their humor, diversity, and the unbreakable bonds of friendship that had been their guiding light from the very beginning.

The summer had been a season of surprises, but the greatest surprise of all was the depth of their friendship and the beautiful complexity of their journey through adolescence in Sunset Park, Brooklyn.

"Teenage Dreams"
Rashidas for your school play
Carlos · Debting · Seera
Delama · Fatiboching · Vontering
Desina · Enima Deking · Sean
Vollernhing · Volintling · De ick
Lei · Anouw · Tech
Dfe Thing
Leavex

6. "Teenage Dreams"

Two more years had swiftly passed, and the group of eight friends, now fifteen years old, found themselves at a pivotal moment in their lives – the transition to high school. Their journey through adolescence had been marked by humor, diversity, and the enduring bonds of friendship, but the challenges and aspirations of their teenage years brought a new layer of complexity to their lives.

Their new high school in Sunset Park was a melting pot of cultures and backgrounds, mirroring the diversity of their neighborhood. As they navigated the maze of hallways on their first day, they could not help but feel a mix of excitement and trepidation.

Alex, always the witty journalist, remarked, "High school, where they expect us to figure out life while we're still trying to open our lockers."

Lei quipped, "Maybe they should offer a 'locker-opening' class."

Their laughter eased the tension, and they continued their journey through the labyrinthine corridors.

Rashida, known for her vibrant slapstick comedy, had already joined the drama club, and was preparing for auditions for the school play. She encouraged her friends to try it out as well, promising them a hilarious and unforgettable experience.

Carlos, the eternal optimist, had set his sights on forming a school band and pursuing his music dreams. He believed that music could bridge cultural gaps and bring people together.

Fatima, balancing family expectations with her personal dreams, had started volunteering at a local clinic, where she assisted doctors and nurses. Her determination to pursue a medical career remained unwavering.

Elena had joined the debate club, using her gift for argumentation to tackle important social issues. Her humor added a unique flair to her speeches.

Sean had become a mentor to younger students, offering guidance and support. His calming presence and humor were a source of comfort to those in need.

Maya continued to explore her identity through her artwork, focusing on themes of culture and diversity. Her creations had gained recognition not only in their school but also in the wider art community.

Their high school experience was a rollercoaster of emotions and self-discovery. As they faced academic challenges, social dynamics, and the complexities of adolescence, their friendship remained a constant source of support and laughter.

One evening, as they gathered at their favorite spot in Sunset Park, they shared their dreams and aspirations for the future. The skyline of Manhattan served as a backdrop to their heartfelt conversations.

Rashida expressed her desire to pursue acting professionally, her eyes shining with determination. "I want to make people laugh, just like we do for each other."

Carlos shared his vision of a multicultural band that would bring different genres and influences together. "Music is our universal language, and I want to create something beautiful with it."

Fatima talked about her dream of becoming a doctor and providing healthcare to underserved communities. "I want to make a difference in people's lives, just like we've made a difference in each other's."

Elena, always quick with a comeback, said, "And I'll be the lawyer who argues for justice and equality. No one can escape my wit and humor in the courtroom."

Sean spoke about his commitment to serving their community as a firefighter. "I want to protect the place we call home, and maybe even rescue a few cats from trees."

Maya shared her passion for creating art that celebrated the beauty of diversity. "I want my art to tell our stories and bring people closer together."

Lei, with her dry humor, added, "And I'll be the tech genius who changes the world, one unexpected invention at a time."

Alex summed it up with a touch of satire, "And I'll be there to write about all your achievements, with plenty of humor and political commentary."

Their dreams were as diverse as their backgrounds, yet they were bound by a common thread – the unwavering support and friendship that had carried them through every stage of life.

Their high school years were marked by academic challenges, late-night study sessions, and the occasional teenage drama. But through it all, they found humor in the most unexpected places, turning stressful moments into opportunities for laughter and bonding.

One memorable incident involved a particularly challenging math exam that had left the entire class in a state of despair. Alex, never one to miss a comedic opportunity, stood up and declared, "Ladies and gentlemen, I present to you the 'Mathemagic' show!" He proceeded to perform comical magic tricks involving calculators and textbooks, earning laughter and applause from his classmates.

Lei, with her tech skills, had once hacked into the school's announcement system to play a surprise birthday message for Carlos during lunch. The unexpected serenade left Carlos blushing and the entire cafeteria in stitches.

Rashida, the actor, had a talent for impersonation, and she often delighted her friends with spot-on imitations of their teachers and classmates. Her ability to mimic their quirks and personalities was a constant source of amusement.

As their high school years passed, their friendship grew deeper and more nuanced. They faced the challenges of self-discovery and identity, navigating the complex terrain of teenage relationships and aspirations. They laughed together, cried together, and supported each other through every triumph and setback.

Their humor and diversity remained the cornerstones of their friendship, a reminder that no matter how much they changed and grew, they would always be the group of eight friends who had embarked on a lifelong journey together in Sunset Park, Brooklyn.

And so, as they looked ahead to the future, they did so with a sense of excitement and curiosity about the adventures and challenges that awaited them. They knew that their friendship would continue to evolve, just as they did individually, but the bonds they had forged in their formative years would remain unbreakable.

Their teenage dreams were as diverse as their backgrounds, but their shared journey was a testament to the enduring power of humor, diversity, and the unbreakable bonds of friendship that had been their guiding light from the very beginning.

7. "Graduation Day"

Two more years had flown by, and the group of eight friends, now seventeen years old, stood on the threshold of a new and exciting chapter in their lives – high school graduation. Their journey through adolescence had been filled with laughter, diversity, and unwavering friendship, and as they gathered in the school courtyard on this momentous day, they could not help but reflect on the path that had led them here.

The courtyard was buzzing with excitement as families, friends, and teachers gathered to celebrate the graduates. The sunbathed the scene in warm, golden light, casting long shadows and painting the world with a sense of transition and anticipation.

Alex could not resist a sarcastic remark. "Well, we made it, folks. Somehow, we survived high school without getting lost in the hallways."

Lei chimed in, "Speak for yourself, Alex. I still get lost in the hallways."

Their laughter echoed through the courtyard, drawing smiles from those around them. Their ability to find humor in even the most nerve-wracking moments was a defining feature of their friendship.

Rashida, known for her vibrant slapstick comedy, decided to add a dose of humor to her graduation attire. She wore oversized, brightly colored sunglasses that had everyone in stitches. "I figured I'd start my acting career with a bang!"

Carlos had decorated his graduation cap with musical notes and a message that read, "Life's a song, and I'm here to dance to its rhythm." His infectious enthusiasm brightened the mood even further.

Fatima, who had successfully balanced family expectations with her personal dreams, delivered a heartfelt speech as the class valedictorian. She spoke about the importance of pursuing one's passions while honoring family values. Her words resonated with many in the audience, and there was not a dry eye in sight.

Elena could not resist adding a touch of wit to her own speech. She quipped, "I'll be the lawyer who argues for laughter as a fundamental human right." Her humor served as a reminder of the group's enduring friendship.

Sean had been selected as the class president, a role he had embraced with grace and humor. His speech centered on unity and the strength of their diverse community. He even managed to sneak in a few firefighter jokes that had everyone chuckling.

Maya had been commissioned to create a mural that adorned one of the courtyard walls. Her artwork depicted the journey of their friendship, from their first day in kindergarten to this momentous graduation day. It was a beautiful celebration of their diversity and bonds.

As they received their diplomas and tossed their caps into the air, they could not help but feel a mix of nostalgia and excitement for the future. Their high school years had been marked by academic challenges, personal growth, and the enduring power of their friendship.

The group of eight friends, whose humor and diversity had defined their journey, gathered for a group photo, their smiles a testament to the bonds they had forged over the years.

After the graduation ceremony, they retreated to their favorite spot in Sunset Park, overlooking the Manhattan skyline. They sat in a circle, their hearts filled with anticipation for the adventures that lay ahead.

Alex mused, "So, what's next for our diverse and humorous group of friends?"

Lei, with her tech expertise, replied, "I plan to explore the tech world and maybe even create a social app for finding lost locker keys."

Rashida said, "I'll keep pursuing my dreams on the stage, and who knows, maybe I'll make it to Broadway one day."

Carlos, ever the optimist, declared, "I'm going to make music that brings people together, no matter where they come from."

Fatima, balancing expectations, and dreams, shared, "I'll continue my journey in medicine, and someday, I hope to provide healthcare to those who need it most."

Elena, the sharp-witted lawyer, smirked, "I'll be the legal eagle who uses humor to win cases and fight for justice."

Sean said, "I'll protect our community as a firefighter and continue to bring people together in times of crisis."

Maya reflected, "I'll create art that celebrates our diversity and tells our stories to the world."

Their dreams were as diverse as their backgrounds, yet their shared journey was a testament to the enduring power of humor, diversity, and the unbreakable bonds of friendship that had been their guiding light from the very beginning.

As they looked ahead to the future, they knew that their paths would diverge, taking them on separate adventures. But their friendship, marked by laughter and diversity, would always remain a cherished part of their lives.

Sunset Park had been their home, their anchor, and the backdrop to their incredible journey. It was a place where humor and diversity thrived, and where their friendship had blossomed into something truly special.

And so, as they watched the sun set over the Manhattan skyline, the group of eight friends felt a sense of gratitude and anticipation for the adventures that awaited them. They knew that no matter where life took them, they would always carry with them the humor, diversity, and the unbreakable bonds of friendship that had been their greatest treasure since that first day in Sunset Park, Brooklyn.

Their graduation day marked not an end but a new beginning, and they faced the future with hearts full of hope, laughter, and the enduring strength of their friendship.

COLLEGE BOUND

8. "College Bound."

Two years had passed since their high school graduation, and the group of eight friends, now nineteen years old, found themselves embarking on a new and exciting adventure – college life. The transition to college was a mix of collegiate exploration and newfound independence, and as they gathered in the bustling courtyard of their university in Sunset Park, Brooklyn, they could not help but feel a sense of anticipation and humor.

Their new college was a melting pot of cultures, ideas, and backgrounds, much like their beloved Sunset Park. As they navigated the sprawling campus on their first day, they were filled with a mix of excitement and nervousness.

Alex, always quick with a witty remark, could not resist commenting on the size of the campus. "I heard college campuses are like mazes, but I didn't expect to need a GPS just to find the cafeteria."

Lei replied, "Maybe we should develop a 'college navigation' app. It's a million-dollar idea."

Their laughter echoed through the courtyard, drawing curious glances from passing students. Their ability to find humor in the most daunting situations was a defining feature of their friendship.

Rashida, known for her vibrant slapstick comedy, had already joined the theater department, and was preparing for auditions for the college play. She encouraged her friends to audition as well, promising them an unforgettable experience.

Carlos had formed a band with fellow students and had started performing at local venues. He believed that music had the power to unite people from all walks of life.

Fatima, balancing family expectations with her personal dreams, had decided to pursue a pre-med track, determined to become a doctor, and make a difference in underserved communities.

Elena had joined the debate team, using her wit and humor to tackle pressing social issues. Her ability to engage in lively debates often left her opponents in stitches.

Sean had become a resident advisor in the dorms, offering guidance and support to younger students. His calming presence and humor continued to be a source of comfort to those in need.

Maya had enrolled in the fine arts program, exploring her identity and heritage through her artwork. Her pieces had gained recognition not only within the university but also in the broader art world.

Their college experience was a whirlwind of academic challenges, newfound friendships, and the pursuit of their dreams. As they faced the complexities of independence and the excitement of collegiate exploration, their friendship remained a constant source of support and laughter.

One evening, as they gathered in their dorm common area, they shared their experiences and aspirations for the future. The common area, adorned with posters, whiteboards, and mismatched furniture, served as the backdrop to their heartfelt conversations.

Rashida expressed her desire to make a name for herself in the theater world, her eyes shining with determination. "I want to bring laughter to Broadway and beyond."

Carlos shared his vision of a multicultural band that would break down barriers through music. "Our band will be a symbol of unity and diversity."

Fatima talked about her journey in medicine and her dream of providing healthcare to underserved communities. "I want to be a doctor who listens and cares for patients, just like we've cared for each other."

Elena, always quick with a witty comeback, said, "And I'll be the lawyer who uses humor to win cases and fight for justice. No one can resist a good laugh."

Sean spoke about his role as a resident advisor and his commitment to building a tight-knit community in the dorms. "I'll be the glue that holds everyone together, one hilarious icebreaker at a time."

Maya reflected, "I'll create art that tells our stories and celebrates our diverse backgrounds. Our journey is a work of art in itself."

Lei, with her dry humor, added, "And I'll be the tech guru who invents gadgets that change the world, one unexpected invention at a time."

Alex summed it up with a touch of satire, "And I'll be there to write about all your achievements, with plenty of humor and political commentary."

Their dreams were as diverse as their backgrounds, yet they were bound by a common thread – the unwavering support and friendship that had carried them through every stage of life.

Their college years were marked by late-night study sessions, lively debates, and the occasional dorm room mishap. But through it all, they found humor in the most unexpected places, turning challenging moments into opportunities for laughter and bonding.

One memorable incident involved a particularly challenging midterm week when stress levels were running high. Alex, never one to miss a comedic opportunity, stood up in the middle of a crowded study session and declared, "Ladies and gentlemen, I present to you the 'Midterm Magic' show!" He proceeded to perform comical magic tricks involving textbooks and flashcards, earning laughter and applause from his fellow students.

Lei, with her tech skills, had once rigged the dorm's speaker system to play a surprise dance party playlist during finals week. The unexpected dance break had everyone grooving to the beat and relieving stress.

Rashida, the actor, had a talent for impersonations and would often entertain her friends with spot-on imitations of their professors and fellow students. Her ability to capture the quirks and personalities of those around them was a constant source of amusement.

As their college years passed, their friendship grew deeper and more nuanced. They faced the challenges of independence and the pursuit of their dreams, all while navigating the complexities of collegiate life.

Their humor and diversity remained the cornerstones of their friendship, a reminder that no matter how much they changed and grew, they would always be the group of eight friends who had embarked on a lifelong journey together in Sunset Park, Brooklyn.

And so, as they looked ahead to the future, they did so with a sense of excitement and curiosity about the adventures and challenges that awaited them. They knew that their friendship would continue to evolve, just as they did individually, but the bonds they had forged in their formative years would remain unbreakable.

Sunset Park had been their home, their anchor, and the backdrop to their incredible journey. It was a place where humor and diversity thrived, and where their friendship had blossomed into something truly special.

As they watched the sun set over the Manhattan skyline from their dorm window, the group of eight friends felt a sense of gratitude and anticipation for the adventures that awaited them. They knew that no matter where life took them, they would always carry with them the humor, diversity, and the unbreakable bonds of friendship that had been their greatest treasure since that first day in Sunset Park, Brooklyn.

Their college years marked not an end but a new beginning, and they faced the future with hearts full of hope, laughter, and the enduring strength of their friendship.

COLLEGE ANGST

9. "College Angst"

Two more years had passed since their college journey began, and the group of eight friends, now twenty-one years old, found themselves facing a new set of challenges and doubts. As they continued their pursuit of dreams, the question of whether they had chosen the right major and elective courses weighed heavily on their minds.

Their university in Sunset Park, Brooklyn, had proven to be both a place of opportunity and a crucible of self-discovery. The campus, bustling with students from all walks of life, was a reflection of the diverse world they had grown up in. As they navigated the complexities of their academic choices, humor and diversity remained their guiding lights.

One sunny afternoon, they gathered in a cozy corner of the university's library, surrounded by towering bookshelves and the hushed whispers of fellow students. The library, with its vast collection of knowledge, served as the backdrop to their discussions and doubts.

Alex, always quick with a sarcastic remark, broke the ice. "So, folks, are we all having a mid-college crisis yet? Wondering if we chose the right majors and electives?"

Lei replied, "I'm still trying to figure out if I chose the right library section. Is 'Tech Gadgets for Dummies' a legitimate elective?"

Their laughter filled the air, earning them amused glances from the studious patrons nearby. Their ability to find humor in the most stressful moments was a testament to their enduring friendship.

Rashida, known for her vibrant slapstick comedy, had recently faced a challenging acting class, and was contemplating her choice of major. "I swear, if I have to do one more dramatic monologue about existentialism, I might spontaneously combust."

Carlos had encountered setbacks in his music career and was questioning his path. "I thought music would be my ticket to success, but it's been a rollercoaster of highs and lows."

Fatima, balancing family expectations with her personal dreams, was struggling with the demands of her pre-med track. "Every day, I ask myself if I'm cut out for this, or if I'm just trying to fulfill someone else's dream."

Elena was immersed in a challenging mock trial and had moments of doubt. "I'm beginning to think that maybe humor isn't the best defense strategy in a courtroom."

Sean had encountered difficulties as a resident advisor and was questioning his role on campus. "Sometimes, I wonder if I'm really making a difference or just dealing with noisy neighbors."

Maya was exploring new themes in her artwork and felt a sense of creative restlessness. "I want my art to evolve, but I'm not sure where it's headed or what it means anymore."

Their doubts and uncertainties were as diverse as their backgrounds, yet they were bound by a common thread – the unwavering support and friendship that had carried them through every challenge in life.

As they shared their concerns and fears, they realized that they were not alone in their college angst. Each one of them had moments of self-doubt, questioning whether they were on the right path. But their friendship, marked by humor and diversity, provided a comforting anchor in the storm of uncertainty.

One evening, after a particularly challenging day of classes and self-reflection, they gathered in their favorite cafe in Sunset Park, a place that had become a sanctuary for their candid conversations.

Alex, the journalist, leaned back in his chair and said, "You know, I've written about politics and satire, but nothing seems as complicated as choosing the right major."

Lei, with her dry humor, replied, "Maybe we should create a 'Life Major' where we learn to adult, make decisions, and find our path."

Their laughter, mingling with the aroma of freshly brewed coffee, drew smiles from the cafe patrons. Their ability to find humor in life's complexities was a testament to their resilience.

Rashida shared her struggle with her acting class and her desire to explore different aspects of theater. "I want to make people laugh, but I also want to challenge myself as an actress."

Carlos talked about his music journey and how he had discovered new genres and influences. "Music is a vast universe, and I want to explore every corner of it."

Fatima admitted that she had moments of self-doubt but was determined to pursue her passion for medicine. "I want to make a meaningful impact on people's lives, even if it means facing challenges along the way."

Elena shared her experiences in mock trials and how she was finding her own unique style in the courtroom. "Humor may not be a traditional defense, but it's my secret weapon."

Sean spoke about the bonds he had formed with students in the dorms and how he had discovered his own sense of purpose. "Sometimes, it's the small moments that make the biggest difference."

Maya talked about her evolving art and how she was exploring new themes and mediums. "Art is a journey of self-discovery, and I'm excited to see where it leads."

Their conversations were filled with honesty, vulnerability, and the reassuring presence of friends who understood the challenges they faced. They realized that college was not just about finding the right major or electives but also about discovering themselves and their individual paths.

As they sipped their coffee and shared their dreams and doubts, they knew that their friendship would continue to be their anchor in the unpredictable sea of college life. The humor and diversity that had defined their journey from the very beginning would remain the constants in their ever-changing lives.

And so, as they looked ahead to the future, they did so with a sense of resilience and camaraderie. They knew that their pursuit of dreams and the challenges they faced were all part of the journey, and that with the support of their diverse and humorous group of friends, they could navigate any uncertainty that college threw their way.

Sunset Park had witnessed their growth, their laughter, and their shared moments of doubt. It was a place where humor and diversity thrived, and where their friendship had evolved into something even more profound.

As they left the cafe and walked back to their dorms, they felt a renewed sense of determination and a deep appreciation for the bonds that had carried them through every twist and turn of their college years. They were not just friends; they were a family, bound by humor, diversity, and the unbreakable bonds of friendship.

Their college angst was not a sign of weakness but a testament to their willingness to confront the uncertainties of life head-on. They knew that, with their friends by their side, they could face any challenge, pursue any dream, and find humor in every moment of doubt.

And so, as they entered the next phase of their collegiate journey, they did so with a sense of optimism, knowing that their friendship would continue to be the guiding star in their pursuit of dreams and the challenges they would face along the way.

10. "College Graduation"

Two years had flown by since their college angst, and now, at the age of twenty-three, the group of eight friends was facing a new set of questions and uncertainties as they prepared to graduate. The pursuit of dreams had led them to this moment, and the challenges of choosing career paths and considering further education weighed heavily on their minds.

Their university in Sunset Park, Brooklyn, had been a place of growth, learning, and unforgettable moments. As they gathered for their graduation ceremony on a sunny day, the campus was abuzz with excitement. It was a culmination of years of hard work, self-discovery, and, of course, humor and diversity.

The graduation ceremony was held in a sprawling outdoor amphitheater, with friends and families gathered to celebrate their achievements. The air was filled with a sense of anticipation and nostalgia as they donned their graduation gowns and caps, ready to step into the next chapter of their lives.

Alex could not resist making a sarcastic comment as they stood in line. "I guess this is it, folks. The real world awaits. Should we start a support group for post-graduation anxiety?"

Lei replied, "I'm already considering a 'Tech Gadgets for Life' course to navigate adulting."

Their banter drew smiles and laughter from their fellow graduates, many of whom recognized them as the group of friends who could always find humor in any situation.

Rashida had been performing in local theater productions and was contemplating her next steps. "I've been doing slapstick comedy for years, but now I'm wondering if it's time to explore more serious roles."

Carlos had faced challenges in the music industry but was determined to pursue his passion. "I've learned that music isn't just about fame; it's about touching people's hearts."

Fatima, balancing family expectations and personal dreams, had completed her pre-med track and was preparing for medical school. "I'm ready to take the next step in my journey to become a doctor, even if it means more years of studying."

Elena had interned at a prestigious law firm and was considering her options. "I've realized that humor can be a powerful tool in the courtroom, but there's still so much to learn."

Sean had continued his role as a resident advisor and had formed deep connections with students. "I want to continue making a difference in the lives of others, one humorous icebreaker at a time."

Maya had highlighted her work in local galleries and was exploring her identity through her art. "Art is my way of expressing who I am and where I come from."

Their individual paths were as diverse as their backgrounds, yet they were bound by a common thread – the unwavering support and friendship that had carried them through every stage of life.

As they walked across the stage to receive their diplomas, they could not help but feel a sense of pride and accomplishment. The years of hard work, late-night study sessions, and shared laughter had led them to this moment.

After the ceremony, they gathered in a nearby park, where a picnic had been arranged to celebrate their graduation. The park, with its lush greenery and the sounds of laughter from families enjoying the day, was the perfect setting for their reunion.

Alex raised his glass and proposed a toast. "To us, the group of friends who have laughed, cried, and grown together. We may not have all the answers, but we have each other."

Lei, with her dry humor, added, "And to the future, where we'll navigate the complexities of adulthood with humor and diversity."

Their laughter echoed through the park, drawing curious glances from other picnickers. It was a moment of pure joy, a testament to the enduring bonds of friendship that had carried them through every challenge in life.

Rashida shared her excitement about pursuing new roles and challenges in the theater world. "I want to explore every facet of acting, from comedy to drama, and everything in between."

Carlos talked about his music journey and how he had formed a band that was gaining recognition in the local music scene. "Music is my passion, and I'm not giving up on my dreams."

Fatima expressed her gratitude for the support of her friends and family as she prepared to enter medical school. "I couldn't have done it without all of you by my side."

Elena shared her experiences from her internship and her plans to continue using humor in her legal career. "I've learned that laughter can break down barriers and make even the toughest cases more manageable."

Sean spoke about the impact he had made as a resident advisor and his plans to continue making a difference in the lives of students. "Our shared sense of humor has the power to create connections and build communities."

Maya talked about her evolving art and how she was using her work to explore her identity and heritage. "Art is a reflection of who we are, and I want to share our stories with the world."

Their conversations were filled with hope, ambition, and the reassurance of friends who had been there for each other every step of the way. They knew that the journey ahead would be filled with challenges and uncertainties, but they also knew that they had the support of their diverse and humorous group of friends.

As the sun began to set over the park, casting a warm, golden glow on their faces, the group of eight friends felt a deep sense of gratitude for the bonds they had forged and the adventures they had shared. They were not just friends; they were a family, bound by humor, diversity, and the unbreakable bonds of friendship.

Their college graduation marked not an end but a new beginning, and they faced the future with hearts full of hope, laughter, and the enduring strength of their friendship. They knew that no matter where life took them, they would always carry with them the humor, diversity, and the unbreakable bonds of friendship that had been their greatest treasure since that first day in Sunset Park, Brooklyn.

11. "The Real World"

Two years had passed since their graduation, and now, at the age of twenty-five, the group of eight friends found themselves facing the harsh realities of adult life. The pursuit of dreams had led them to various corners of the world, but the challenges of job hunting, financial independence, and the complexities of adulthood were universal.

Sunset Park, Brooklyn, had been their home for many years, but now they had scattered to different cities and countries, chasing their respective careers and dreams. Despite the physical distance, their friendship remained as strong as ever, and they made it a point to gather whenever possible.

On a crisp autumn evening, they found themselves reunited in their beloved Sunset Park. The park, with its vibrant foliage and the sounds of children playing, was a nostalgic reminder of their shared childhood. It was the perfect setting for their reunion.

As they sat on a bench, overlooking the park's serene lake, Alex, always quick with a sarcastic remark, could not help but comment on the challenges of adulting. "So, who else is feeling the weight of student loans and the pressure to 'adult'?"

Lei replied, "I thought adulting would involve more exciting things, like spontaneous road trips and gourmet cooking. Instead, it's all about bills and budgeting."

Their banter drew laughter from the group, a reminder that humor was their constant companion in navigating life's challenges.

Rashida had faced auditions and rejections in the competitive world of theater but remained determined to follow her dreams. "I've been told 'no' more times than I can count, but I won't give up on what I love."

Carlos had experienced setbacks in his music career but continued to create music that resonated with his audience. "Music is my passion, and I'll keep making it, no matter the obstacles."

Fatima had embarked on her medical residency, a demanding journey that tested her resolve. "Every day is a challenge, but I'm committed to becoming the best doctor I can be."

Elena had faced her share of courtroom battles and was known for her fierce advocacy. "Humor may not win cases, but it keeps me sane in a world of legal jargon."

Sean had encountered the realities of firefighting, from saving lives to battling intense blazes. "It's a tough job, but it's worth it to make a difference in people's lives."

Maya had highlighted her work in galleries around the world, exploring themes of identity and heritage. "Art is a journey of self-discovery, and I'm on an endless quest to find my voice."

Their individual journeys were as diverse as their backgrounds, yet they were bound by a common thread – the unwavering support and friendship that had carried them through every stage of life.

As they shared their experiences and challenges, they realized that they were not alone in facing the complexities of adulthood. Each one of them had encountered moments of self-doubt and uncertainty, but their friendship, marked by humor and diversity, provided solace in the face of life's storms.

One evening, after a long day of work and responsibilities, they gathered at their favorite neighborhood pizzeria, a place that had witnessed countless celebrations and heart-to-heart conversations.

Alex raised his glass and proposed a toast. "To us, the group of friends who have weathered the storm of adulthood with humor and diversity. We may not have it all figured out, but we have each other."

Lei, with her dry humor, added, "And to the future, where we'll continue to navigate the complexities of life one sarcastic comment at a time."

Their laughter and clinking glasses filled the pizzeria, drawing smiles from the other diners. It was a moment of camaraderie, a reminder that no matter where life took them, they could always count on their diverse and humorous group of friends.

Rashida shared her recent audition experiences and the moments of self-doubt that came with rejection. "I've learned that success in theater is about resilience and unwavering passion."

Carlos talked about his music journey and how he had found inspiration in unexpected places. "Music has a way of bringing people together, and I want to keep sharing my music with the world."

Fatima shared stories of the patients she had encountered during her medical residency. "Every day, I'm reminded of the impact I can make in people's lives, and it keeps me going."

Elena spoke about her courtroom victories and the challenges she faced as a young attorney. "Humor may not win cases, but it's a powerful tool for building connections with clients."

Sean talked about the bonds he had formed with his fellow firefighters and the sense of purpose he found in his work. "Saving lives is a responsibility I take seriously, and I'm proud to be part of a dedicated team."

Maya shared her experiences of traveling and immersing herself in different cultures, which had influenced her artwork. "Art is a universal language, and I want to use it to bridge gaps and celebrate diversity."

Their conversations were filled with empathy, understanding, and the reassuring presence of friends who had been there for each other every step of the way. They knew that adulthood came with its share of challenges, but they also knew that they had the support of their diverse and humorous group of friends.

As they left the pizzeria and walked through the familiar streets of Sunset Park, they felt a deep sense of gratitude for the bonds they had forged and the adventures they had shared. They were not just friends;

they were a family, bound by humor, diversity, and the unbreakable bonds of friendship.

The real world had tested their resilience, but it had also strengthened their friendship. They knew that no matter what lay ahead, they could face it with the humor, diversity, and the unbreakable bonds of friendship that had been their greatest treasure since that first day in Sunset Park, Brooklyn.

12. "Career Beginnings"

Two years had passed since their reunion in Sunset Park, and now, at the age of twenty-seven, the group of eight friends found themselves navigating the turbulent waters of early career struggles and triumphs. The pursuit of dreams had led them on different professional paths, each filled with its own set of challenges and opportunities.

Their diverse backgrounds and unique perspectives continued to be a source of strength and humor as they gathered for a weekend brunch in a cozy café in Sunset Park. The café's warm ambiance and the aroma of freshly brewed coffee created the perfect setting for their reunion.

As they settled into their seats, Alex could not help but comment on the ups and downs of their careers. "So, who else is juggling deadlines, demanding bosses, and the occasional existential crisis?"

Lei replied, "I thought I was tech-savvy until my computer crashed during a video conference with my boss. I had to resort to sign language to explain the problem."

Their banter drew laughter from the group, a reminder that humor was their constant companion in navigating the complexities of the professional world.

Rashida had secured a role in a popular sitcom, and her vibrant slapstick comedy had garnered her a dedicated fan base. "I'm living my dream, but the hours on set can be grueling. Who knew making people laugh could be so exhausting?"

Carlos had faced career challenges in the music industry but had recently released a hit single that was climbing the charts. "It's been a rollercoaster ride, but I'm finally seeing the fruits of my labor."

Fatima had completed her medical residency and was now working at a busy hospital. "The long shifts can be draining, but I'm committed to making a difference in patients' lives."

Elena had become known for her tenacity in the courtroom, winning several high-profile cases. "I've learned that humor can be a powerful tool in negotiations, and I'm not afraid to use it."

Sean had faced challenging situations as a firefighter but had also saved lives and received commendations for his bravery. "Every day brings new challenges, but I'm honored to serve my community."

Maya had continued to explore themes of identity and heritage in her artwork, gaining recognition in the art world. "Art is a journey of self-discovery, and I'm on a lifelong quest to express my roots."

Their individual journeys were as diverse as their backgrounds, yet they were bound by a common thread – the unwavering support and friendship that had carried them through every stage of life.

As they shared their experiences and challenges, they realized that their careers were not just about success but also about personal growth and resilience. Each one of them had encountered moments of self-doubt and triumph, but their friendship, marked by humor and diversity, provided a stable anchor in the ever-changing professional landscape.

One evening, after a long day of work and responsibilities, they gathered at Elena's apartment, which had become their unofficial meeting place for heart-to-heart conversations.

Alex raised his glass and proposed a toast. "To us, the group of friends who have navigated the treacherous waters of early careers with humor and diversity. We may not have it all figured out, but we have each other."

Lei, with her dry humor, added, "And to the future, where we'll continue to tackle professional challenges with our unique blend of humor and resilience."

Their laughter and clinking glasses filled the apartment, a testament to their enduring friendship and their ability to find humor even in the face of adversity.

Rashida shared stories from the set of her sitcom and the camaraderie she had formed with her fellow actors. "We may work long hours, but we're like a family on and off-screen."

Carlos talked about the joy of performing on stage and connecting with his audience through music. "I've learned that perseverance and a positive attitude can open doors."

Fatima shared her experiences of making life-altering decisions in the emergency room. "Every day, I'm reminded of the importance of compassion and empathy."

Elena spoke about her recent courtroom victories and the pride she felt in advocating for her clients. "Humor may not be the only tool, but it certainly lightens the mood."

Sean talked about the bonds he had formed with his fellow firefighters and the sense of camaraderie that defined their profession. "We face danger together, but we also share moments of triumph."

Maya shared her creative process and how she used art to explore her identity and connect with others. "Art has the power to bridge cultures and create understanding."

Their conversations were filled with empathy, understanding, and the reassuring presence of friends who had been there for each other every step of the way. They knew that the professional world could be challenging, but they also knew that they had the support of their diverse and humorous group of friends.

As they left Elena's apartment that night, they felt a deep sense of gratitude for the bonds they had forged and the adventures they had shared. They were not just friends; they were a family, bound by humor, diversity, and the unbreakable bonds of friendship.

Their early career struggles had tested their resilience, but they had emerged stronger and more determined. They knew that no matter what lay ahead, they could face it with the humor, diversity, and the unbreakable bonds of friendship that had been their greatest treasure since that first day in Sunset Park, Brooklyn.

13. "Love and Loss"

Two years had passed since their last reunion, and now, at the age of twenty-nine, the group of eight friends found themselves navigating the complexities of romantic relationships and heartbreaks. The pursuit of love and the challenges of maintaining relationships were the new frontiers they were exploring, each with their own unique experiences and stories to share.

Their diverse backgrounds and unique perspectives continued to be a source of strength and humor as they gathered for a picnic in Sunset Park. The park's lush greenery and the soothing sound of the breeze through the leaves created the perfect backdrop for their reunion.

As they spread out their picnic blankets and unpacked their food, Alex, always quick with a sarcastic remark, could not help but comment on the ups and downs of love. "So, who else has experienced the joys of love and the heartaches of heartbreak?"

Lei replied, "I once sent a 'love you' text to my boss instead of my date. Needless to say, it was a memorable first date."

Their banter drew laughter from the group, a reminder that humor was their constant companion in navigating the complexities of love and relationships.

Rashida had found herself in a whirlwind romance with a fellow actor, but their careers often kept them apart. "Love in the spotlight can be intense, but it also comes with its share of challenges."

Carlos had experienced the thrill of falling in love, but his music career had led him to travel frequently, putting a strain on his relationship. "Long-distance love tests the strength of the heart."

Fatima had met someone who understood the demands of her medical career, but they faced the dilemma of when to start a family. "Life and love are a delicate balance, and sometimes, choices are not easy."

Elena had been on her fair share of dates but had yet to find someone who could match her wit. "Humor is a double-edged sword in dating. It either creates a connection or sends them running."

Sean had met a fellow firefighter who shared his passion for saving lives, but their demanding schedules made it challenging to spend time together. "Being in the same profession helps us understand each other's commitments."

Maya had explored themes of love and identity through her artwork, drawing inspiration from her own experiences. "Art has a way of expressing emotions that words cannot."

Their individual love stories were as diverse as their backgrounds, yet they were bound by a common thread – the unwavering support and friendship that had carried them through every stage of life.

As they shared their experiences and challenges, they realized that love was a journey filled with surprises, joy, and heartbreak. Each one of them had encountered moments of bliss and disappointment, but their friendship, marked by humor and diversity, provided comfort in the face of love's uncertainties.

One evening, after a day of laughter and heartfelt conversations, they gathered around a bonfire in Maya's backyard. The crackling flames and the starry sky created a magical atmosphere for sharing their stories.

Alex raised his glass and proposed a toast. "To us, the group of friends who have braved the highs and lows of love with humor and diversity. We may not have all the answers, but we have each other."

Lei, with her dry humor, added, "And to the future, where we'll continue to explore the mysteries of the heart with our unique blend of humor and resilience."

Their laughter and clinking glasses filled the night, a testament to their enduring friendship and their ability to find humor even in matters of the heart.

Rashida shared tales of romantic escapades and the challenge of balancing her career with her personal life. "Love can be a whirlwind, but I'm learning to find my footing."

Carlos talked about the power of love to inspire his music and the lessons he had learned about the importance of communication. "Love songs come from the heart, and so should conversations."

Fatima spoke about the conversations she had with her partner about the future and the compromises they were willing to make. "Love is about making choices and facing them together."

Elena shared humorous anecdotes from her dating experiences and the moments when her wit had either charmed or baffled her dates. "Love requires a sense of humor, especially when the bill arrives."

Sean talked about the challenges of maintaining a relationship with someone who understood the demands of his profession. "We may not see each other as often as we'd like, but we cherish the moments we have."

Maya shared her creative process and how love had influenced her artwork, capturing the essence of human connection. "Love is a muse that never fails to inspire."

Their conversations were filled with empathy, understanding, and the reassuring presence of friends who had been there for each other every step of the way. They knew that love could be both beautiful and complicated, but they also knew that they had the support of their diverse and humorous group of friends.

As they left Maya's backyard that night, they felt a deep sense of gratitude for the bonds they had forged and the adventures they had shared. They were not just friends; they were a family, bound by humor, diversity, and the unbreakable bonds of friendship.

Love and loss had tested their hearts, but they had emerged with a deeper understanding of themselves and the enduring power of friendship. They knew that no matter what lay ahead in matters of the heart, they could face it with the humor, diversity, and the unbreakable bonds of friendship that had been their greatest treasure since that first day in Sunset Park, Brooklyn.

14. "Reunion"

Two years had passed since their last gathering, and now, at the age of thirty-one, the eight friends found themselves back in Sunset Park, Brooklyn, for their high school reunion. It was a chance to reminisce about old times, catch up on each other's lives, and see how everyone had changed over the years.

The school's courtyard, bathed in the soft glow of fairy lights, was the perfect setting for their reunion. As they entered the courtyard, memories of their time in school flooded back. The laughter, the pranks, and the shared experiences had forged a bond that had withstood the test of time.

Alex could not resist poking fun at their younger selves as they stood in front of the school building. "Remember when we thought we were the coolest kids in school?"

Lei replied, "I still think I'm cool, but my social interactions haven't improved much."

Their banter drew laughter from the group, a reminder that their sense of humor remained unchanged.

Rashida could not help but reenact some of the slapstick comedy routines they had performed during their school talent shows. "I may have grown up, but the comedian in me is still alive and kicking."

Carlos, ever the optimist, looked around at his friends and said, "I always knew we'd achieve great things, and here we are, proving it."

Fatima, who had successfully balanced family expectations with her personal dreams, smiled and added, "Our journey hasn't been easy, but we've come a long way."

Elena could not resist commenting on the school's decor. "They've certainly upgraded since our time here. Maybe they should hire me as their legal counsel."

Sean reminisced about their adventures as teenagers. "We may have had our differences, but we always had each other's backs."

Maya marveled at the diversity of their group. "We come from different backgrounds, but that's what makes us special."

As they entered the school building, they were greeted by their former teachers and classmates. It was a chance to reconnect with old acquaintances and share stories of their journeys since graduation.

Their interactions with other attendees highlighted their ability to connect with people from all walks of life, a skill they had honed over the years. Alex's political satire had the teachers in stitches, Lei's dry humor broke the ice with former classmates, and Rashida's slapstick comedy brought back memories of their school talent shows.

Carlos's optimism and musical talent had everyone tapping their feet, while Fatima's empathetic nature made her a great listener for those sharing their life stories. Elena's sharp wit and legal expertise made her the center of attention in discussions, while Sean's peacemaking skills diffused any tense moments. Maya's artistic expression through her work provided a source of inspiration and conversation.

As the night went on, they found themselves gathered in the courtyard, sharing stories from their journeys into adulthood. The challenges they had faced, the triumphs they had celebrated, and the lessons they had learned were all part of the tapestry of their lives.

Alex, always the journalist, had uncovered a scandal in the world of politics that had earned him recognition and a fair share of enemies. "Political satire may have its risks, but it's a powerful tool for change."

Lei, who had excelled in the tech world, had overcome her struggles with social interactions and was now leading a team of innovators. "Sometimes, you have to embrace your quirks to find success."

Rashida had landed a role in a hit comedy series, and her vibrant slapstick comedy had become her signature. "Laughter is the universal language that connects us all."

Carlos, who had faced career challenges in music, had found his niche as a songwriter and producer, creating music that resonated with audiences. "Sometimes, the detours lead you to your true calling."

Fatima, who had balanced family expectations and personal dreams, had become a respected doctor, and was involved in medical missions around the world. "Family support is essential, but so is staying true to yourself."

Elena had made partners at her law firm and had taken on high-profile cases. "A sharp wit and a compassionate heart can go a long way in the legal world."

Sean had been promoted to captain of the fire department and was known for his leadership and dedication. "Being a firefighter is not just a job; it's a calling."

Maya had her work displayed in galleries across the country, exploring themes of identity and diversity. "Art has the power to bridge gaps and bring people together."

Their stories were a testament to their growth and resilience, and they could not help but feel a sense of pride in each other's achievements. The diversity of their backgrounds had enriched their lives and had become a source of strength and humor throughout their journey.

As the night drew to a close, they gathered in a circle, their hands joined in unity. They knew that their friendship was a rare and precious gem, one that had withstood the test of time and had grown stronger with each passing year.

Alex, with his trademark wit, summed it up perfectly. "We may have changed over the years, but one thing remains constant – our friendship and our ability to find humor in every situation."

Lei, with her dry humor, added, "And our knack for turning diversity into our greatest strength."

Rashida, with a twinkle in her eye, exclaimed, "Here's to us, the friends for life, who have laughed, cried, and celebrated together."

Carlos, with his eternal optimism, raised his glass. "And to many more reunions and adventures in the years to come."

Fatima, with her empathetic nature, said, "Our friendship is a treasure, and I'm grateful for each and every one of you."

Elena, with her sharp wit, chimed in, "May our bond continue to grow, and may we always find humor in the journey of life."

Sean spoke from the heart. "Through thick and thin, we've stood by each other, and that's what makes us a family."

Maya captured the moment with her words. "Our diversity is our strength, and our friendship is our legacy."

Their laughter and heartfelt moments echoed through the courtyard, a testament to the enduring power of their friendship. As they left the reunion that night, they knew that no matter where life took them, they had a group of friends who would always be there to celebrate their successes, support them in their challenges, and find humor in every moment of their journey.

15. "Midlife Musings"

As the eight friends entered their mid-thirties, they found themselves facing the inevitable midlife crises, career peaks, and family dynamics that came with the territory. Their journey had taken them from the schoolyard in Sunset Park to the bustling streets of New York City, and they had weathered it all with their trademark humor and diversity.

They had gathered at a local cafe in Brooklyn, a familiar spot where they had spent countless hours chatting, debating, and sharing their dreams. The atmosphere was cozy, with the scent of freshly brewed coffee filling the air.

Alex, ever the journalist, could not help but poke fun at their advancing years. "Well, folks, we're officially in our mid-thirties. It is time for us to buy convertibles and start calling it a 'midlife crisis.'"

Lei retorted, "I have been practicing my 'I'm too cool for this' look in the mirror for years. I'm ready for my crisis."

Their banter was as lively as ever, a testament to their enduring friendship.

Rashida had a new role in a Broadway play and was known for her vibrant slapstick comedy. "I may be getting older, but my physical comedy skills are still top-notch."

Carlos had faced career challenges in music but had finally found success as a songwriter and producer. "It took a while, but I've learned that the detours in life often lead to the best destinations."

Fatima, who had successfully balanced family expectations with her personal dreams, was now a respected doctor with a thriving practice. "Sometimes, it's about finding the right balance and staying true to yourself."

Elena had taken on high-profile cases and was known for her wit in the courtroom. "The legal world may be tough, but so am I."

Sean had been promoted to battalion chief at the fire department and was admired for his leadership. "Being a firefighter is not just a job; it's a calling, and I'm proud to serve."

Maya had her work displayed in galleries worldwide, exploring themes of identity and diversity. "Art has the power to change perspectives and bring people together."

Their diverse backgrounds had enriched their lives, and their ability to find humor in every situation had been their guiding light. They had faced challenges, celebrated successes, and supported each other through it all.

As they sipped their coffee, they delved into the topic of family dynamics. Alex, with his penchant for political satire, could not resist a humorous take on parenthood. "You know you're getting older when your idea of a wild night is watching Netflix past 9 PM without falling asleep."

Lei, who had excelled in the tech world, shared her struggles with balancing her career and family life. "Tech may be my expertise, but balancing work and family is a whole different challenge."

Rashida had recently become a mother and marveled at the joys and chaos of parenthood. "Motherhood is a rollercoaster, but it's the most rewarding role I've ever had."

Carlos had started a family of his own and could not help but reflect on the journey. "Life has thrown its curveballs, but I wouldn't change a thing."

Fatima, the empathetic doctor, had her hands full with both her medical practice and her growing family. "Sometimes, I feel like I'm juggling a million things, but I wouldn't have it any other way."

Elena shared her insights into navigating the complexities of relationships. "Communication and humor are key, even in the toughest of times."

Sean had a family of his own and spoke of the importance of balance. "Being a firefighter and a father has taught me the value of time and presence."

Maya explored the theme of family and identity through her work. "Family shapes our identity in profound ways, and it's a theme I'll always explore."

Their conversations were a blend of humor, reflection, and shared experiences. They knew that midlife brought its challenges, but they were determined to face them with the same resilience and unity that had defined their friendship.

As they left the cafe that evening, they walked through the streets of Brooklyn, their laughter and camaraderie echoing through the night. They knew that their journey was far from over, and they looked forward to whatever the future held, knowing that their humor, diversity, and enduring friendship would continue to be their greatest legacy.

16. "Parenting Perils"

In their mid-thirties, life had taken yet another twist for the eight friends. Parenthood had become the new adventure, bringing with it a unique blend of humor and chaos. As they gathered in their favorite Brooklyn cafe, the air was filled with the excitement and trepidation that came with being parents.

Alex, always the one to inject humor into any situation, could not resist poking fun at their newfound roles as parents. "Well, it looks like we've officially entered the world of diaper changes and sleepless nights. Who would have thought?"

Lei, the tech-savvy one of the group, chimed in with her dry, unexpected humor. "I've programmed robots to do some pretty complicated tasks, but nothing prepared me for a toddler's tantrum algorithm."

Their laughter echoed through the cafe, drawing amused glances from other patrons.

Rashida, known for her vibrant slapstick comedy, had become a mother, and was navigating the ups and downs of parenthood. "I've perfected the art of juggling toys, bottles, and pacifiers while attempting to maintain my sanity."

Carlos was embracing fatherhood with open arms, even though his music career had faced its share of challenges. "Music might not pay all the bills, but the sound of my baby's laughter is worth more than any record deal."

Fatima shared stories of her experiences as a mother, balancing family expectations with her personal dreams. "Being a pediatrician definitely comes in handy when dealing with my own kids, but they still manage to keep me on my toes."

Elena had her hands full with a toddler and a demanding legal career. "Cross-examining a toddler's 'why' questions should be an Olympic sport. They never run out of 'whys.'"

Sean had become a father and was known for his patience and ability to diffuse any situation. "I've learned that negotiating with a toddler is like negotiating a hostage situation—only with more snacks involved."

Maya found inspiration in her children and explored themes of identity and family in her work. "Watching my kids discover their own identities is a constant source of inspiration for my art."

Their conversations were a whirlwind of anecdotes, parenting advice, and shared frustrations. They had come to realize that parenthood was a journey filled with both laughter and challenges, and their diversity had become an asset in understanding the unique needs of their children.

As they sipped their coffee and shared stories, they found solace in the fact that they were not alone in their parenting perils. They were a tight-knit group, bound by years of friendship and the shared experience of navigating the unpredictable world of parenthood.

Outside the cafe, they watched as their children played together in a nearby park, their laughter blending with the memories of their own childhood. The circle of life continued, and they faced each new chapter with their trademark humor and diversity, knowing that their enduring friendship would see them through any challenge life had in store.

Parenthood brought its fair share of surprises and challenges, and the friends navigated them with their signature humor and camaraderie. They swapped stories of sleepless nights, temper tantrums, and the endless pursuit of that elusive work-life balance.

Alex, who had always been known for his wit and sarcasm, found that his quick humor was now put to the test during bedtime routines. "Trying to convince a toddler that bedtime is a good thing is like negotiating a peace treaty with a stubborn dictator."

Lei, the tech whiz, brought her problem-solving skills to the world of parenting. "I've created spreadsheets for everything from diaper changes to baby food preferences. It's all about data analysis now."

Rashida, the actor, turned her knack for drama into entertaining bedtime stories. "My son thinks I'm the best storyteller in the world. Little does he know; I'm just winging it most of the time."

Carlos found joy in the simplest moments with his child. "Watching my daughter take her first steps was like winning a Grammy. I've never been prouder."

Fatima, the doctor, applied her medical knowledge to every cough and sniffle. "I can diagnose a common cold from a mile away. Motherhood has turned me into a medical detective."

Elena, the lawyer, became the go-to mediator during sibling disputes. "I've settled more arguments over toys than I have in the courtroom. It's a different kind of negotiation."

Sean used his calming presence to soothe fussy babies. "I've learned the art of the baby whisperer. Sometimes, all it takes is a gentle lullaby."

Maya captured the beauty of parenthood through her artwork. "My kids have become my muses. Every painting tells a story of our journey together."

Their diverse backgrounds and personalities enriched their parenting experiences. They embraced each other's differences and leaned on their friendship for support during the challenging moments.

Despite the sleepless nights and chaotic days, their laughter remained a constant presence in their lives. They celebrated each other's parenting victories, no matter how small, and offered a shoulder to lean on during the tough times.

As they watched their children grow and develop their own unique personalities, they could not help but feel a sense of wonder and gratitude. Parenthood had brought them closer together, and they cherished the moments they shared as both friends and parents.

Their high school reunion had been a nostalgic trip down memory lane, but it also served as a reminder of how much they had grown and evolved over the years. They had faced the challenges of adulthood head-on, relying on their humor and diversity to navigate the complexities of life.

As they sat around the table, sipping on their coffees and sharing stories of parenthood, they could not help but feel a deep sense of contentment. They had come a long way from their kindergarten days in Sunset Park, but their friendship had remained a constant source of strength and support.

In the midst of the chaos and unpredictability of parenthood, they had discovered a profound sense of joy and fulfillment. Their children were a reflection of the love and laughter that had defined their friendship for so many years.

As the sun set over Sunset Park, casting a warm glow over the cafe, they raised their cups in a toast to friendship, parenthood, and the beautiful journey of life that they were all experiencing together.

17. "Old Friends, New Paths"

Time had a way of molding and shaping the lives of the eight friends who had grown up together in Sunset Park. As they entered their late thirties, their journeys had taken unexpected turns, leading them down diverse paths. The group's dynamics had evolved, but their unwavering bond remained at the core of their friendship.

One sunny afternoon, they gathered at their favorite park, reminiscing about their shared history while savoring the present moment. They had always been a source of laughter and support for each other, and this day was no different.

Alex, the journalist with a sharp wit, had found his passion project in political satire. He had a growing following for his humorously scathing takes on current events. As he sipped his coffee, he quipped, "Who would've thought my sarcastic comments in kindergarten would turn into a career?"

Lei, the tech-savvy genius, had embarked on a new venture. She was developing a groundbreaking social app designed to help people connect on a deeper level. "It's ironic," she mused, "that someone who once struggled with social interactions is now trying to bring people closer together."

Rashida had achieved her dream of performing on Broadway. She had become known for her versatility in both drama and comedy. "Life is a stage, and I'm here to deliver the best performance I can," she declared, her eyes sparkling with passion.

Carlos had faced career challenges in the music industry. But he had discovered fulfillment in teaching music to underprivileged youth. "Sometimes, the best way to find your path is to help others find theirs," he shared, a smile lighting up his face.

Fatima had started her own medical clinic focused on providing care to underserved communities. "I've learned that the greatest impact we can have is by caring for those who need it most," she said, her dedication evident in every word.

Elena had taken on high-profile cases that challenged the status quo. She was known for her unwavering commitment to justice. "The courtroom is where I fight for what's right," she stated, her voice filled with determination.

Sean had been promoted to lieutenant in the fire department. He had become a mentor to younger firefighters, teaching them the importance of unity and camaraderie. "Saving lives is not just about putting out fires; it's about being there for each other," he explained.

Maya had embarked on a journey of self-discovery, exploring her Afro-Latina heritage through her work. Her paintings were a vibrant reflection of her identity. "Art has always been my way of understanding who I am," she shared, her eyes shining with creativity.

Their individual paths had led them in different directions, but their friendship remained the bedrock of their lives. They embraced each other's passions and celebrated their successes, finding joy in the diversity of their experiences.

As they sat in the park, their laughter and conversation echoed through the trees, drawing curious glances from passersby. They shared stories of their trials and triumphs, offering support and encouragement to one another.

Elena, with her trademark wit, could not resist poking fun at their evolving dynamics. "Remember when we were just a bunch of kids causing chaos in the schoolyard?"

Alex, always quick with a comeback, replied, "Ah, those were the days. Now we're just a bunch of adults causing chaos in the real world."

Their laughter filled the air, a testament to the enduring power of their friendship. They had grown older, wiser, and more diverse in their pursuits, but they were still the same group of friends who had bonded over humor and diversity in kindergarten.

As the sun began to set over Sunset Park, casting a warm glow over their gathering, they raised their cups in a toast. Their paths might have diverged, but their friendship remained unwavering, a source of strength and joy that had withstood the test of time.

The years had brought changes and challenges, but through it all, they had remained a constant in each other's lives. Their friendship was a reflection of the diverse, complex, and beautiful journey they had all undertaken, and they could not wait to see where life would take them next.

Their conversations often turned to their dreams and aspirations, and they found solace in the fact that despite their different paths, they were still a source of inspiration and support for one another. Alex, who had always been the witty and sarcastic one, now used his humor to shed light on the absurdities of the political landscape. His satirical articles and commentary had garnered a dedicated following, and he relished the opportunity to use his words to make a difference.

Lei had found her niche in the tech world, despite her earlier struggles with social interactions. Her app aimed to bridge the gap between people, encouraging meaningful connections in an increasingly digital age. She often chuckled at the irony of her journey, saying, "I guess I had to overcome my own challenges to create something that brings people together."

Rashida's career had soared to new heights as she continued to captivate audiences with her performances. She had become known for her ability to seamlessly transition between dramatic roles and slapstick comedy, earning accolades and adoration from fans and critics alike. "It's all about finding the balance between laughter and tears," she would say with a mischievous grin.

Carlos, who had once dreamt of musical stardom, had discovered a different kind of fulfillment as a music teacher. He poured his heart into nurturing young talents, imparting not only musical skills but also life lessons about perseverance and passion. "My students inspire me as much as I inspire them," he mused.

Fatima's medical clinic had become a beacon of hope for the underserved communities in Sunset Park. She had managed to strike a balance between her family's expectations and her own dreams of making a meaningful impact on people's lives. "Sometimes, you have to create your own path," she would tell her friends.

Elena continued to champion justice in the courtroom, taking on cases that challenged the status quo. Her sharp mind and unwavering determination had earned her the respect of both her peers and opponents. "Every case is a chance to make a difference," she would say, her eyes filled with conviction.

Sean, the firefighter turned lieutenant, had become a pillar of strength within the department. He took pride in mentoring the next generation of firefighters, emphasizing the importance of camaraderie and unity in their life-saving mission. "We're not just a team; we're a family," he would tell his recruits.

Maya's art had evolved to become a powerful exploration of her Afro-Latina heritage and identity. Her paintings were a testament to her journey of self-discovery, each brushstroke representing a piece of her soul. "Art has a way of connecting us to our roots," she would explain to anyone who asked.

Their individual pursuits had led them to diverse and fulfilling careers, but their bond remained as strong as ever. They continued to meet regularly, sharing their triumphs and challenges, and offering unwavering support to one another.

As they sat in the park that sunny afternoon, the world around them seemed to fade into the background. Their laughter, camaraderie, and shared history were the focal points of the day. They toasted to their friendship, each raising a cup in appreciation of the years they had spent together.

Elena, always quick with her witty remarks, could not resist poking fun at the changing dynamics of their group. "Remember when we were just a bunch of kids causing chaos in the schoolyard?"

Alex, with his trademark sarcasm, replied, "Ah, those were the days. Now we're just a bunch of adults causing chaos in the real world."

Their laughter rang out, a testament to the enduring power of their friendship. They had grown older, wiser, and more diverse in their pursuits, but they were still the same group of friends who had bonded over humor and diversity in kindergarten.

As the sun began to set over Sunset Park, casting a warm, golden glow over their gathering, they knew that their friendship would continue to be a source of strength and joy in the years to come.

They had weathered the storms of life together, celebrating each other's successes and providing a shoulder to lean on during the tough times. Their friendship was a reflection of the diverse, complex, and beautiful journey they had all undertaken, and they could not wait to see where life would take them next.

The years had brought changes and challenges, but through it all, they had remained a constant in each other's lives. Their friendship was a testament to the enduring power of humor, diversity, and the unbreakable bonds forged in the crucible of childhood.

As they left the park that evening, they knew that their journeys were far from over. They had faced the trials of adulthood together, and they were ready to tackle whatever the future held, armed with the strength of their friendship and the knowledge that they were not alone on this incredible journey called life.

18. "Coming Home"

Sunset Park had always held a special place in the hearts of the eight friends who had grown up together there. It was where their friendship had blossomed, where they had shared countless memories, and where they had become the people, they were today. Two years after their last gathering, a significant event brought them all back to the neighborhood, reigniting old connections and filling their hearts with joy.

The occasion was Rashida's Broadway debut in a leading role. She had come a long way from her days of performing slapstick comedy in school. Her talent had shone brightly, earning her the opportunity to grace the grand stage of a prestigious theater. As the night of her debut approached, the excitement among the group was palpable.

Alex could not help but tease Rashida about her newfound fame. "Remember when you used to trip over your own feet in the school hallway? Now you are the star of Broadway!"

Rashida, with her infectious laughter, replied, "Well, I guess I've learned how to stay on my feet, at least on stage!"

Lei, the tech genius with a dry sense of humor, chimed in, "Don't worry, Rashida. If anything goes wrong, I'll build a robot to save the day."

Carlos, ever the optimist, added, "And I'll provide the musical backdrop for your triumphant robot rescue!"

Fatima could not contain her excitement. "I'm so proud of you, Rashida. You've come a long way, and your talent deserves to be celebrated."

Elena, the sharp-tongued lawyer with a heart of gold, smiled warmly. "It's moments like these that make us appreciate the journey we've all been on."

Sean, the firefighter, and peacemaker of the group raised his glass to a toast. "To Rashida, the shining star of Sunset Park!"

Maya, the artist exploring her identity through her work, had created a stunning painting as a gift for Rashida. It depicted a vibrant theater marquee with Rashida's name in dazzling lights. "Your journey is an inspiration to us all," she said, presenting the artwork with pride.

As the night of Rashida's debut drew near, the group eagerly anticipated the performance. It was a testament to the enduring bond they shared that they had all made the effort to return to Sunset Park for this special occasion.

On the night of the performance, the marquee of the theater shone brightly, casting a warm glow on the bustling crowd that had gathered to support Rashida. The group took their seats, their hearts filled with anticipation.

Rashida's performance was nothing short of mesmerizing. She commanded the stage with a presence that left the audience spellbound. Her vibrant energy and comedic timing drew uproarious laughter, while her dramatic moments moved many to tears.

Backstage, after the final curtain call, Rashida was greeted by her friends with hugs, tears, and laughter. They congratulated her on a performance that had left a lasting impact on everyone present.

As they gathered at a nearby restaurant to celebrate, the atmosphere was filled with joy and camaraderie. They recounted their favorite moments from the performance, with Alex offering humorous commentary and Lei adding her dry, unexpected observations.

Carlos, who had once dreamt of musical stardom, shared, "Rashida, you've achieved something incredible tonight. Your talent has brought so much joy to all of us."

Fatima, who had balanced family expectations with her own dreams, added, "You've shown us that with dedication and passion, we can all reach for the stars."

Elena, always the voice of reason, raised her glass. "To Rashida, who reminds us that dreams are worth pursuing, no matter where life takes us."

Sean clinked his glass with a smile. "And to the enduring friendship that has brought us all back to this special place."

Maya, who had explored her own identity through her art, had one final surprise for Rashida. She presented a small sculpture she had crafted, representing the essence of Rashida's journey. "Your talent is a work of art in itself," she said.

Rashida, touched by the love and support of her friends, could not hold back her tears of gratitude. "You all mean the world to me. Sunset Park will forever be the place where our dreams took flight."

As the night continued, their laughter echoed through the restaurant, drawing the curious gazes of other patrons. It was a testament to the enduring power of their friendship, humor, and diversity.

They had come full circle, returning to Sunset Park to celebrate Rashida's success and their unbreakable bond. The years had brought them diverse paths and experiences, but they had always found their way back to each other, united by the enduring connection forged in their childhood.

As they left the restaurant that night, their hearts were full, and their spirits were lifted. Rashida's debut had been a momentous occasion, but more importantly, it had brought them all back to their roots, reminding them of the joy of coming home.

The years had taught them that life was a journey filled with ups and downs, but with the support of true friends, it was a journey worth taking. Their laughter and shared memories were a testament to the enduring power of friendship, and they could not wait to see what the future held for them.

As they walked through the familiar streets of Sunset Park, their footsteps echoed with the echoes of their childhood. They were no longer the children who had once caused chaos in the schoolyard, but they were still the same group of friends who had laughed, cried, and celebrated together for decades.

Sunset Park had been the backdrop to their lives, witnessing their growth, their challenges, and their triumphs. It was a place that held their memories, their dreams, and their enduring bond. And as they walked together through its streets, they knew that no matter where life took them, Sunset Park would always be their home.

The years had been kind to them, and they had been kind to each other. Their friendship had weathered the tests of time, growing stronger with each passing year. As they looked at the stars that lit up the Brooklyn night sky, they knew that their journey was far from over.

With laughter in their hearts and the support of their dearest friends, they were ready to face whatever challenges and joys the future held. Sunset Park, with its rich tapestry of memories, would always be the place where their story began, and they would forever cherish the bonds they had forged in that vibrant neighborhood.

As they said their goodbyes that night, promising to meet again soon, they knew that their friendship was a treasure beyond measure. They were no longer just friends; they were family, bound by love, humor, and the enduring magic of Sunset Park. And with that, they walked into the night, ready to face the adventures that awaited them in the next chapter of their lives.

19. "Reflections and Regrets"

Life had a way of moving forward, and the friends from Sunset Park were no exception. Two years had passed since their last reunion, and now they found themselves at a crossroads, contemplating their past decisions, unfulfilled dreams, and the weight of their regrets. Parenthood had brought new perspectives, and the bonds of friendship remained as strong as ever.

It was a sunny weekend afternoon when they all gathered at Elena's newly purchased family home in Sunset Park. The house had a warm, inviting aura, with a spacious backyard where their children played. Elena had mellowed over the years, but her wit remained as sharp as ever.

As they sat on the porch, sipping iced tea and reminiscing about their youth, the topic turned to their dreams and the paths they had taken in life. It was Alex, the political satirist, who broke the silence with a self-deprecating quip. "You know, I always thought I'd be a famous journalist by now, exposing the political absurdities of the world. Instead, I'm just the guy who writes quirky columns for a local newspaper."

Lei, the tech wizard, leaned back in her chair and chuckled. "Well, at least you have a job. I sometimes wonder if I should have pursued those social interaction classes instead of computer science. I mean, who knew techies would become social icons?"

Rashida, who had found success in her acting career, shared her thoughts. "I may be living my dream on Broadway, but there are times when I wonder if I missed out on other aspects of life, like having a family."

Carlos, always the optimist, chimed in, "I may not be the next big music sensation, but I've made some great music with my family."

Fatima, balancing her demanding career as a doctor with motherhood, sighed. "Sometimes, I wonder if I could have done more with my art. My parents wanted me to be a doctor, but there was always a painter inside me."

Elena, the homeowner, spoke up, "I used to think I'd become a high-powered lawyer in a corner office, but I wouldn't trade my family for any amount of success."

Sean, who had dedicated his life to firefighting and community service, reflected, "I've saved lives and helped people, but there's a part of me that still wants to do more."

Maya, the artist exploring her identity through her work, shared her perspective. "Art has been my salvation, but there are days when I wonder if I could have made a bigger impact."

As the conversation unfolded, it became clear that each of them carried their own regrets and unfulfilled dreams. Yet, they also realized that the choices they had made had led to meaningful lives filled with love, family, and friendship.

Elena's young daughter ran up to the group, holding a crayon drawing. "Look, Mommy, I drew you and your friends!" she exclaimed.

The drawing depicted the eight friends sitting on the porch, their laughter and camaraderie beautifully captured by the child's innocent hand. It was a poignant reminder that their friendship had spanned generations, and the children who played in the backyard were a testament to the legacy they were building.

With tears in her eyes, Elena hugged her daughter tightly. "You're absolutely right, sweetheart. These are the best friends a person could have."

The children's laughter and the embrace of friendship filled the air, washing away the weight of their regrets. They may not have achieved all their childhood dreams, but they had found something equally precious—their place in each other's lives.

As the sun set over Sunset Park, they knew that life was a tapestry of choices, regrets, and unfulfilled dreams, but it was also a canvas where they could paint new memories, share old stories, and cherish the bonds that had endured the test of time.

With humor, diversity, and a deep understanding of each other's journeys, they faced the uncertainties of the future with the knowledge that their friendship would always be a source of strength and joy. They were no longer the children who had once run through the schoolyard, but they were still the same friends who had laughed, cried, and celebrated together for a lifetime.

And as they gathered on the porch, watching their children play and the stars twinkle in the Brooklyn sky, they could not help but feel grateful for the shared moments that had made their lives richer and their friendships stronger. Sunset Park had been the backdrop to their journey, and it would always be the place where their story continued to unfold.

The years had taught them that regrets were a part of life, but they were also a reminder of the roads not taken. It was in those unfulfilled dreams that they found the motivation to cherish the present and pursue new aspirations. Together, they faced the future with humor, diversity, and the enduring bonds of friendship, knowing that no matter what challenges lay ahead, they would always have each other to lean on.

As the night deepened, they exchanged stories and laughter, celebrating the beauty of the moment and the promise of tomorrow. The porch of Elena's home had witnessed the passage of time and the evolution of their lives, but it had also become a sanctuary of friendship, where they could always come together to reflect, share, and find solace in each other's company.

With hearts full of love, they knew that their friendship was a treasure beyond measure, and as they looked at the Brooklyn skyline, they whispered their hopes and dreams to the stars, knowing that their journey was far from over. Together, they had weathered the storms of life, and they were ready to embrace whatever adventures awaited them in the next chapter of their lives.

With the warmth of friendship to guide them, they knew that they could face any challenge, conquer any regret, and find joy in the simplest moments. Sunset Park was not just a place on the map; it was the heart of their story, and it was where they had built a legacy of humor, diversity, and enduring friendship.

As they said their goodbyes that night, they knew that their bond was unbreakable, and they looked forward to the chapters that still lay ahead. The porch lights cast a warm glow on their faces, and as they walked away, their laughter echoed through the neighborhood, a testament to the enduring power of friendship.

Sunset Park had seen them through childhood, adolescence, and adulthood, and it would continue to be the place where they gathered to celebrate, reflect, and find solace in each other's presence. Theirs was a story of resilience, humor, diversity, and the unwavering bonds of friendship, and they would not have it any other way.

With hearts full of gratitude, they knew that their journey was far from over. The porch of Elena's home had witnessed countless memories and conversations, and it would continue to be the place where they came together to share their lives, dreams, and regrets.

And as the night embraced Sunset Park, they looked ahead with hope and anticipation, knowing that they had each other to lean on, to laugh with, and to face the uncertainties of life. The legacy they were building was one of love, humor, diversity, and the enduring strength of their friendship, and it was a legacy that would carry them through the years to come.

The end of one chapter marked the beginning of another, and the friends from Sunset Park were ready to face the future with open hearts and a deep appreciation for the journey they had shared. As they walked away from Elena's home, the Brooklyn night whispered its secrets to them, promising that their story was far from over.

With humor, diversity, and a bond that could withstand the test of time, they knew that the road ahead would be filled with both challenges and triumphs. But one thing was certain—no matter where life took them, Sunset Park would always be their home.

The years had been kind to them, and they had been kind to each other. Their friendship had weathered the tests of time, growing stronger with each passing year. As they looked at the stars that lit up the Brooklyn night sky, they knew that their journey was far from over.

With laughter in their hearts and the support of their dearest friends, they were ready to face whatever challenges and joys the future held. Sunset Park, with its rich tapestry of memories, would always be the place where their story began, and they would forever cherish the bonds they had forged in that vibrant neighborhood.

As they said their goodbyes that night, promising to meet again soon, they knew that their friendship was a treasure beyond measure. They were no longer just friends; they were family, bound by love, humor, and the enduring magic of Sunset Park. And with that, they walked into the night, ready to face the adventures that awaited them in the next chapter of their lives.

20. "Our children are bonding."

Two years had passed since the last gathering of the friends from Sunset Park, and life had continued to unfold in its unpredictable ways. They had seen each other through career successes and adversities, personal growth, and the joys and challenges of parenthood. Now, in their early forties, they were about to experience something that would further cement their bonds.

It was a sunny Saturday morning, and the group had decided to meet at the local community center in Sunset Park. As they arrived one by one, the familiar faces greeted each other with warm hugs and laughter.

Alex, the quick-witted journalist, was the first to arrive. "Well, well, look who's here! The gang's all back together."

Lei, with his dry and unexpected humor, quipped, "I heard we were meeting here, so I figured I'd bring my tech wizardry to the party."

Rashida, always the vibrant one, burst into laughter. "Tech wizardry? Lei, you're about as tech-savvy as a cat with a typewriter."

Carlos chimed in, "Come on, guys, let's not start with the teasing already. We're here for something special."

Fatima, balancing her medical career and motherhood, nodded in agreement. "Carlos is right. We have something important to share."

Elena, the sharp-tongued lawyer with a heart of gold, raised an eyebrow. "Well, don't leave us in suspense. What is this big secret?"

Sean, the firefighter, and peacemaker of the group, smiled. "It's not a secret, but it's definitely exciting. Our children are bonding."

Maya, the artist who explored identity through her work, added, "That's right. Our kids have been getting to know each other and forming their own friendships. It's like history repeating itself."

As they settled into a circle of chairs in the community center, they could not help but feel a sense of nostalgia. It was as if they had come full circle, returning to the place where their own friendships had blossomed.

Rashida's daughter, Olivia, a talented young actor with a flair for comedy, was the first to arrive. She greeted the group with a dramatic flourish and a bright smile.

Lei's son, Ethan, a tech-savvy teenager with a penchant for robotics, followed soon after. He nodded to everyone with a shy smile, his eyes darting between the adults and the electronic gadget he was fiddling with.

Carlos's daughter, Sofia, an aspiring singer with a love for music, arrived with a cheerful greeting. She carried a guitar case, eager to show off her latest composition.

Fatima's son, Aryan, a thoughtful young man with a passion for art, joined the group with a sketchbook in hand. He shyly showed them a drawing he had been working on.

Elena's daughter, Anya, a sharp-minded and precocious child, confidently joined the circle. She greeted them with a playful wink, her wit and intelligence shining through.

Sean's twin daughters, Emma, and Liam brought a burst of energy to the group. They were full of laughter and mischief, just like their father.

Maya's son, Rafael, a budding artist like his mother, approached with a sense of quiet curiosity. He carried a sketchpad, his eyes filled with the same creative spark that had always defined their group.

As the children settled into the center of the circle, the adults could not help but exchange knowing glances. They had watched their kids grow from infants to toddlers and now into young individuals with their own personalities and interests.

Alex could not resist making a witty comment. "Well, it looks like the next generation of Sunset Park's finest is ready to take over the world."

Lei chuckled. "If they're anything like us, they'll certainly make their mark."

Rashida beamed with pride. "I can already tell Olivia is destined for the stage. She's got the same spark in her eyes."

Carlos ruffled Sofia's hair affectionately. "And my little singer here is ready to serenade the world."

Fatima nodded, glancing at Aryan's sketch. "Aryan's artistry is truly something special. He's inherited your talent, Maya."

Elena raised an eyebrow at Anya. "Our lawyer in the making, perhaps?"

Sean laughed as Emma and Liam chased each other around the circle. "These two are a handful, but they've got the firefighter spirit in them."

Maya watched Rafael with a smile. "He's got a unique perspective on life, just like his mom."

The children, oblivious to the conversation around them, were already forming their own bonds. Olivia was teaching Ethan a dramatic monologue, while Sofia and Aryan were discussing music and art. Anya, Emma, and Liam had formed a mini-drama troupe, and Rafael was sharing his sketching techniques with his new friends.

As the adults observed their children interacting with humor, diversity, and a sense of camaraderie, they could not help but feel a deep sense of pride and happiness. These young friendships were a testament to the enduring legacy of their own bond.

Alex turned to Lei and said, "You know, we may have our careers and challenges, but seeing our kids here, making friends and finding their passions, it's a pretty wonderful feeling."

Lei nodded; her dry humor momentarily replaced by genuine emotion. "You're right, my friend. Our children are creating their own memories in Sunset Park, just like we did."

Rashida chimed in, "And who knows what the future holds for them? Maybe one day, they'll be sitting in this very community center, reminiscing about their own adventures."

Carlos grinned, his optimism shining through. "Whatever they choose to do, I know they'll have each other's backs, just like we always have."

As the day wore on, the children continued to bond, their laughter filling the community center. The adults watched with a sense of fulfillment, knowing that their legacy of friendship, humor, and diversity was being passed down to a new generation.

And as they left the community center that day, the friends from Sunset Park could not help but feel a profound sense of contentment. They had faced career successes and adversities, navigated the complexities of adulthood, and now, they were witnessing the beautiful cycle of life as their children forged their own friendships.

Sunset Park had always been their home, and the bonds they had formed there would forever be a source of strength, support, and joy. With humor, diversity, and the enduring power of friendship, they were ready to face whatever the future held, knowing that their legacy would continue to flourish in the hearts of their children and the generations to come.

21. "Rekindling Passions"

Two years had passed since the group had gathered to celebrate their children's budding friendships. Life had continued to evolve, and the friends from Sunset Park were now in their mid-forties, facing the familiar challenges of empty nest syndrome. With their children away pursuing their own adventures, the adults found themselves with newfound free time, and they decided it was time to rekindle forgotten hobbies and passions.

One crisp autumn afternoon, they met at a cozy café in Sunset Park. The air was filled with the rich aroma of freshly brewed coffee, and the warm chatter of friends filled the room.

Alex, always quick with a sarcastic remark, raised his cup of coffee. "Well, folks, here's to rediscovering the joys of life without the kids hanging around."

Lei, with her dry humor, added, "I never thought I'd miss the chaos of my son's robotics experiments, but here we are."

Rashida, known for her vibrant slapstick comedy, could not help but chuckle. "I've been rehearsing monologues in an empty living room. It's just not the same."

Carlos grinned. "My guitar has been gathering dust in the corner. It's time to change that."

Fatima, who had balanced her medical career with family life, nodded in agreement. "I've been thinking about volunteering at the local clinic. It's something I used to love."

Elena, the sharp-tongued lawyer with a heart of gold, sipped her tea. "I might take up painting. It's a good way to channel my thoughts."

Sean, the firefighter, and peacemaker, leaned back in his chair. "I've been meaning to learn a new instrument. Maybe the bagpipes."

Maya, the artist who explored identity through her work, smiled. "I've got a whole studio of unfinished projects. Time to get back to them."

As they chatted, it became evident that they were all eager to rekindle their passions and hobbies. They had spent years supporting each other through life's challenges and milestones, and now it was their turn to focus on themselves.

Lei, ever the tech enthusiast, took out his tablet. "I've been thinking about starting a blog, sharing my adventures in tech and social interaction. Maybe it'll help others like me."

Alex raised an eyebrow. "A blog, Lei? You might actually become famous for your quirky humor."

Rashida nodded enthusiastically. "I could use your tech skills, Lei. Maybe we can create some online comedy sketches."

Carlos strummed an imaginary guitar. "And I'll provide the soundtrack. We could start a virtual band."

Fatima smiled. "I'll volunteer at the clinic and also write a medical blog. It'll be great to give back and share knowledge."

Elena could not resist a teasing remark. "Well, if you're writing a blog, Fatima, I might start a legal advice column. We can compete for readers."

Sean laughed. "And I'll learn the bagpipes online, documenting my progress. Maybe we can have a virtual jam session."

Maya's eyes sparkled with excitement. "I'll create an online gallery for my artwork. It's time to share my journey with the world."

As they made plans to pursue their passions, it was evident that their humor and diversity were as strong as ever. They were each on unique paths, but their friendship remained a constant source of support and inspiration.

In the weeks that followed, they delved into their newfound hobbies with enthusiasm. Lei's blog on tech and social interactions gained a dedicated following, and she even started a podcast with Rashida, exploring the lighter side of technology.

Carlos, inspired by his friends, composed music for their online comedy sketches and found himself rediscovering his love for songwriting.

Fatima's medical blog provided valuable information to readers, and she also organized free health clinics in the community, fulfilling her desire to give back.

Elena's legal advice column became a hit, and she found herself helping people navigate legal challenges with her signature sharp wit.

Sean's bagpipe playing improved with each practice session, and he started giving online lessons, connecting with aspiring musicians around the world.

Maya's online gallery highlighted her artwork, and she even collaborated with Lei and Rashida on a virtual art and comedy project that gained a dedicated online following.

As they pursued their passions and rediscovered their talents, their bond as friends remained unbreakable. They continued to meet at their favorite café, sharing stories of their adventures and laughing at the quirks of life.

One evening, as they sat together, enjoying the warmth of friendship and the aroma of coffee, Alex spoke up, his voice tinged with nostalgia. "You know, it's funny how life has a way of coming full circle. We started as a group of friends exploring the world together, and now we're back to pursuing our passions with the same enthusiasm."

Lei nodded, a rare sentimental expression on her face. "It's true. Our paths may have taken different turns, but our friendship has remained constant."

Rashida chimed in, "And I wouldn't have it any other way. You guys are the family I chose."

Carlos raised his coffee cup. "To rediscovering passions and living life to the fullest."

Fatima added, "And to the enduring power of friendship."

Elena, always quick with a clever remark, concluded, "Here's to us, the Sunset Park adventurers, still exploring the world, one passion at a time."

With humor, diversity, and the unwavering support of one another, they continued their journey through life, eager to see where their passions would lead them next. And as they pursued their dreams, their laughter filled the air, a testament to the enduring bonds of friendship that had carried them through every chapter of their lives.

22. "Changing Times."

The friends from Sunset Park had entered their late forties, and the world around them was evolving at a rapid pace. The neighborhood they had known and loved was changing, gentrification creeping in like an unwelcome guest. As they gathered once again at their favorite café, they could not help but notice the alterations in their beloved community.

Alex, sipping his coffee with a wry smile, could not resist a sarcastic remark. "Well, it seems Sunset Park has decided to become the 'hipster' capital of Brooklyn. I feel like an outsider in my own neighborhood."

Lei, always quick with her dry humor, quipped, "I tried to explain a meme to a neighbor the other day, and they looked at me like I was speaking a foreign language. Maybe I am."

Rashida, known for her slapstick comedy, mimicked a highbrow tone. "Darling, I attended a neighborhood meeting, and they were discussing the intricacies of artisanal kale farming. I nearly fell off my chair."

Carlos sighed. "The bodegas that once played salsa music all night are now selling avocado toast. Times are changing, my friends."

Fatima, who had balanced her medical career with family life, nodded in agreement. "Even the local clinic has been replaced by a high-end spa. It's like a different world."

Elena raised an eyebrow. "I saw a group of young professionals debating the ethical implications of avocado toast pricing. It's madness."

Sean, the firefighter, and peacemaker, leaned back in his chair. "The firehouse is now surrounded by organic food stores. The irony is not lost on me."

Maya, the artist exploring identity through her work, sighed. "The art scene has become so commercial. It's all about trends and branding now."

As they chatted, they couldn't help but feel a sense of nostalgia for the Sunset Park they had known. A different kind of diversity was replacing the neighborhood's diversity and vibrancy – one that came with a price tag.

Alex, ever the journalist, could not help but delve deeper. "I've been thinking about writing an article on the changing face of Sunset Park. It's a story that needs to be told."

Lei nodded. "I'm with you, Alex. Maybe we can use technology to bridge the gap between the old and new residents."

Rashida, in her colorful way, added, "And I'll organize a community theater performance to remind everyone of the neighborhood's history."

Carlos, inspired by his friends, thought aloud, "I can write songs that capture the essence of the old Sunset Park, a musical tribute."

Fatima smiled. "I'll host health workshops for the community, reminding them of the importance of accessible healthcare."

Elena, always ready for a legal challenge, quipped, "I'll handle any legal disputes that arise from this gentrification process."

Sean, ever the community-oriented firefighter, chimed in, "I'll organize a neighborhood barbecue, bringing everyone together."

Maya's eyes sparkled with determination. "I'll create art that reflects the changing times, a visual representation of our community's resilience."

As they made plans to preserve the essence of their neighborhood, they realized that their humor and diversity were essential in the face of these changing times. They were united by a shared love for Sunset Park and a determination to ensure that its heart and soul remained intact.

In the weeks that followed, their projects took shape. Alex's article highlighted the stories of long-time residents, bridging the gap between old and new neighbors.

Lei's tech initiatives brought together residents from different backgrounds, creating a sense of community in the digital age.

Rashida's community theater performance was a hit, reminding everyone of the neighborhood's vibrant history.

Carlos's songs celebrated the diversity and resilience of Sunset Park, capturing the spirit of the place they all loved.

Fatima's health workshops were well-received, offering valuable knowledge to the community.

Elena's legal expertise helped protect the rights of long-time residents facing displacement.

Sean's neighborhood barbecue brought people together, fostering a sense of unity.

Maya's artwork served as a visual reminder of the neighborhood's changing face and the strength of its people.

As they worked tirelessly to preserve their community's essence, they realized that their friendship was a source of strength. They might not be able to stop gentrification entirely, but they could ensure that the Sunset Park they had known and loved continued to exist in the hearts of its residents.

One evening, as they sat together at their favorite café, Alex raised his coffee cup. "To our Sunset Park, a place where diversity and humor thrive even in changing times."

Lei, ever the tech enthusiast, added, "And to using technology to bridge the gaps between generations."

Rashida, with her theatrical flair, declared, "Here's to preserving the stories and memories that make this neighborhood special."

Carlos, strumming an imaginary guitar, chimed in, "To the music that unites us and reminds us of our roots."

Fatima, always the voice of reason, said, "And to the importance of accessible healthcare and education for all."

Elena, with her sharp wit, concluded, "Here's to fighting for justice and ensuring that the Sunset Park we love endures."

Sean raised his glass. "To community and unity, no matter how much the world around us changes."

Maya's eyes shone with passion. "And to art, the universal language that captures the essence of our ever-evolving neighborhood."

With humor, diversity, and unwavering determination, they continued to face the evolving world and the challenges of gentrification. Sunset Park might be changing, but with their bonds of friendship, they were determined to leave their mark on their beloved community, ensuring that its heart remained intact, no matter how much the world around them evolved.

23. "Legacy"

As the friends from Sunset Park celebrated their milestone anniversary at a familiar café, they could not help but reflect on the legacy they wanted to leave behind. Their faces carried the marks of time, but their spirits were as lively as ever. Their conversations were seasoned with humor and diversity, just as they had always been.

Alex, with a knowing grin, raised his coffee cup. "Well, my friends, here's to us. Forty-nine and still cracking jokes like teenagers. If that's not a legacy, I don't know what is."

Lei, who had come a long way in embracing social interactions, replied with her dry humor, "And here I thought I'd retire as a tech recluse. Who knew I'd be having coffee with all of you."

Rashida, always the vivacious one, chimed in, "Legacy, huh? I am thinking of starting a comedy school for underprivileged kids. Teaching them to find humor in life's challenges."

Carlos nodded enthusiastically. "Count me in, Rashida. I want to create a music program for local youth, helping them navigate the tricky waters of the music industry."

Fatima, balancing her medical career with personal dreams, added, "I'm considering starting a foundation that provides scholarships for aspiring doctors from diverse backgrounds."

Elena, the sharp-tongued lawyer with a heart of gold, raised an eyebrow. "I'll offer legal support to those who can't afford it. Ensuring that justice is not a privilege."

Sean, the peacemaker, and community-oriented firefighter smiled warmly. "I'll continue organizing neighborhood events that bring people together. Unity is our strength."

Maya's eyes sparkled with passion. "I want to create public art installations that celebrate our community's diversity and resilience."

As they shared their aspirations, they realized that their legacy was not just about individual achievements but about the impact they could have on the world around them. Their friendship had always been a source of strength, and now it was the foundation on which they would build their legacies.

In the weeks that followed, they began to put their plans into action. Alex's articles highlighted the work of his friends, inspiring others to get involved in community projects.

Lei's tech expertise helped streamline the operations of their initiatives, making them more efficient and accessible.

Rashida's comedy school brought laughter and joy to the lives of underprivileged children, teaching them to find humor even in difficult circumstances.

Carlos's music program provided young musicians with the guidance and mentorship they needed to navigate the competitive music industry.

Fatima's foundation started awarding scholarships to aspiring doctors, breaking down barriers to entry in the medical field.

Elena's legal support ensured that everyone had access to justice, regardless of their financial circumstances.

Sean's neighborhood events continued to foster a sense of unity and community among Sunset Park residents.

Maya's art installations served as a visual reminder of the neighborhood's diversity and resilience, inspiring others to celebrate their heritage.

As the years passed, their legacies grew, and the impact of their work became evident in the community. Sunset Park, once facing gentrification and change, had found its strength in the bonds of friendship and the determination to leave a positive mark on the world.

One evening, as they sat together at their favorite café, Alex raised his coffee cup. "To our legacies, my friends. May they continue to inspire and uplift the generations to come."

Lei, with her dry humor, added, "And may we continue to find humor in life's challenges, no matter how old we get."

Rashida, the vibrant soul, declared, "Here's to laughter, music, and art, the universal languages that bring us all together."

Carlos chimed in, "To making a difference, one small act of kindness at a time."

Fatima, the voice of reason, said, "And to breaking down barriers and providing opportunities for those who need them."

Elena, always ready for a legal challenge, concluded, "Here's to justice, equality, and the pursuit of a better world for all."

Sean raised his glass. "To community and unity, the pillars of our strength."

Maya's eyes shone with passion. "And to art, the mirror that reflects the beauty of our diversity."

With humor, diversity, and an unwavering commitment to their legacies, they continued to make a difference in Sunset Park and beyond. They knew that their friendship was the greatest legacy of all, one that would continue to inspire generations to come.

24. "Golden Celebrations"

It was a crisp autumn day in Sunset Park, and the friends for life were gathered at a local park, surrounded by colorful leaves and a golden sunset. They had come together to celebrate a significant milestone – their 51st birthdays. Laughter and joy filled the air as they shared stories, jokes, and cherished memories.

Alex, with his trademark wit, began the festivities. "Well, well, my friends, here we are, officially in our fifties. Who would have thought we would survive this long with our humor and diversity intact?"

Lei, now a successful tech entrepreneur but still struggling with social interactions, quipped, "Speak for yourself, Alex. I'm still not sure how I made it this far without short-circuiting."

Rashida, the life of the party as always, exclaimed, "Fifty-one looks good on us! I have slapstick comedy routines planned for each of you tonight!"

Carlos raised his glass. "Here's to music, my friends, the one thing that has always kept me going, no matter the challenges."

Fatima, the doctor balancing family expectations, and personal dreams, smiled warmly. "And here's to health, happiness, and finding the perfect balance in life."

Elena, the sharp-tongued lawyer with a heart of gold, added, "To justice, equality, and continuing to make a difference in our community."

Sean, the peacemaker, and community-oriented firefighter, said, "To the bonds of friendship that have only grown stronger over the years."

Maya, her passion for art still burning bright, declared, "To creativity, identity, and the power of self-expression."

As they toasted to their shared journey and the years ahead, they could not help but reflect on the chapters of their lives that had brought them to this moment. Their friendship had been a constant source of strength, humor, and diversity, and it had carried them through the highs and lows of life.

The park was adorned with decorations, and a live band played music that spanned the decades of their friendship. People from all walks of life joined their celebration, a testament to the impact they had on their community.

Throughout the evening, they danced, sang, and laughed together. Rashida's slapstick comedy routines had everyone in stitches, and Carlos's impromptu music performance got everyone on their feet. Fatima shared stories of her medical career, Elena defended a passionate argument, and Sean organized an impromptu community gathering around a bonfire.

As the night grew darker, Maya's art installations illuminated the park, casting a warm and colorful glow over their gathering. The laughter and camaraderie continued well into the early hours of the morning.

As the sun began to rise, they gathered one last time around a bonfire, their faces reflecting the golden light of dawn. Alex, the wordsmith, spoke up. "To another year of friendship, humor, and diversity. We may be in our fifties, but our spirits are forever young."

Lei, with her dry humor, added, "And just think, in another fifty years, we'll have even more material for our jokes."

Rashida, the ever-enthusiastic one, exclaimed, "Here's to never losing our zest for life, no matter how old we get!"

Carlos raised his guitar. "To music, the language that transcends time and age."

Fatima, the voice of reason, smiled. "And to the wisdom that comes with each passing year."

Elena, with her sharp tongue and golden heart, said, "To standing up for what's right and making a lasting impact."

Sean declared, "To unity, community, and the bonds that hold us together."

Maya's eyes shone with passion. "And to art, the mirror that reflects the beauty of our journey."

As they celebrated their golden years, the friends for life knew that their journey was far from over. With renewed purpose, they would continue to give back to their community, inspire those around them, and live their lives to the fullest. Their legacy was not just about what they had accomplished; it was about the joy, laughter, and love they had shared along the way.

25. "Loss and Resilience"

The group gathered under the clear night sky, a cool breeze rustling through the trees in Sunset Park, Brooklyn. A somber air hung over them as they sat in a circle, their faces etched with grief and sadness. They had come together not for a celebration, but to mourn the loss of one of their own, a dear friend who had been a constant presence in their lives.

Sean, the Irish-American firefighter who had always been the group's peacemaker, had passed away unexpectedly. It had been a shock to everyone, a reminder of the fragility of life, and the pain of losing someone they had considered invincible.

As they sat in silence, memories of Sean flooded their minds. His hearty laughter, his unwavering support, and his ability to diffuse any tense situation with his humor were the qualities they cherished the most. He had been the glue that held their diverse group together, the one who always brought a smile to their faces.

Elena, the sharp-tongued Russian-Jewish lawyer, spoke first, her voice quivering with emotion. "Sean was more than just a friend; he was a brother to me. He had this incredible gift of making us all feel like family. We will miss him deeply."

Rashida, the aspiring African-American actor known for her vibrant slapstick comedy, wiped away her tears. "He was the kindest soul I've ever known. Sean was always there, supporting my dreams, and making us laugh even in the toughest times."

Fatima, the Pakistani-American doctor who had balanced family expectations with personal dreams, added, "Sean's presence was a source of comfort for all of us. He had this unique ability to bring people together, to make us appreciate the beauty of diversity."

Maya, the Afro-Latina artist who had explored her identity through her work, chimed in, "He showed us that our differences were what made us special, that our unique backgrounds enriched our lives. Sean was a true friend to all of us."

As each friend shared their memories and feelings, they began to find solace in the collective grief. Lei, the Chinese-American tech whiz who had a dry, unexpected sense of humor, spoke up. "Sean always said that life was too short to hold grudges, to waste time on trivial matters. We should honor his memory by living our lives to the fullest."

Carlos, the Puerto Rican musician who had faced career challenges with optimism and naivety, nodded in agreement. "He taught us to find joy in the simplest things, to appreciate the beauty in everyday moments. We can't let his spirit fade away."

Alex, the witty and sarcastic journalist of Greek descent who loved political satire, offered a small smile. "Sean was a beacon of positivity in our lives. Let's keep that flame alive, for him and for each other."

They spent the evening reminiscing about their adventures, their inside jokes, and the countless times Sean had brought them together. They realized that even in his absence, his legacy of friendship, humor, and unity would continue to shape their lives.

In the weeks that followed, the group leaned on each other for support. They organized a memorial service that celebrated Sean's life, filled with laughter and stories that captured his essence. It was a fitting tribute to their friend who had always brought them together through humor and diversity.

Though the pain of loss remained, they knew that Sean's spirit would forever be a part of their lives. His lessons in unity, joy, and the beauty of diversity would continue to guide them as they faced the challenges and changes that life brought their way.

And so, as they sat together under the starry night sky in Sunset Park, they found strength in their shared grief, knowing that their bond was unbreakable, even in the face of loss. Sean's legacy lived on in their hearts, a reminder that true friendship could withstand the test of time and adversity.

26. "Retirement Reflections"

Age: 55 2 years AFTER Sean's passing.

As the years had rolled on, the group of friends had experienced countless adventures, challenges, and losses together. Their bonds had grown stronger, and now, they were facing a new chapter in life: retirement. The setting was, as always, Sunset Park in Brooklyn, where their journey had begun.

Alex, the witty and sarcastic journalist of Greek descent, could not help but crack a joke as they sat on a bench overlooking the park. "So, retirement, huh? Does that mean we finally get to sleep in and watch daytime TV?"

Lei, the female Chinese-American tech whiz known for her dry humor, responded with a smirk, "Well, Alex, at least you won't have to deal with those early morning editorial meetings anymore."

Rashida, the African-American aspiring actor known for her vibrant slapstick comedy, chimed in, "I'm just excited to not have to memorize lines or wear those crazy costumes anymore. Retirement means sweatpants all day, every day!"

Carlos, the Puerto Rican musician who had faced career challenges with optimism and naivety, laughed heartily. "I'll miss performing, but hey, I can finally focus on that album I've been talking about for years."

Fatima, the Pakistani-American doctor who had balanced family expectations with personal dreams, sighed with relief. "No more double shifts at the hospital. I'm looking forward to some well-deserved relaxation."

Elena, the sharp-tongued Russian-Jewish lawyer with a heart of gold, raised an eyebrow. "Retirement doesn't mean I'll stop arguing with everyone, right? Because that's a hard habit to break."

Maya, the Afro-Latina artist who had explored her identity through her work, grinned. "I'll have more time for my art, and maybe even some new projects. Retirement feels like a blank canvas waiting to be filled."

As they shared their hopes and plans for retirement, Sean's absence was keenly felt. His presence had always been a source of comfort and wisdom. His passing had reminded them of the preciousness of time and the importance of cherishing each moment.

Lei, with her practical nature, spoke up, "Have any of you thought about what we'll do with all this free time? Retirement planning should include more than just napping and gardening."

Alex raised an eyebrow. "Are you suggesting we form a retirement club, Lei?"

Lei's eyes twinkled with mischief. "Why not? We can explore new hobbies, volunteer, travel, or even start a community project."

Rashida, always the creative one, clapped her hands. "I love the idea! We can put our diverse skills and backgrounds to good use."

Carlos nodded enthusiastically. "Count me in. Retirement doesn't mean we stop making a difference in our community."

Fatima, who had always juggled family and career, smiled. "It's a chance to rediscover ourselves, our passions, and maybe even reinvent our lives."

Elena, true to form, could not resist a witty comment. "Well, if we're going to start a club, I suggest we have regular debates. Retirement isn't an excuse to stop using our brains."

Maya added her unique perspective. "And we can use our creativity to make a lasting impact, leaving behind a legacy for future generations."

The group had always thrived on their diversity, their humor, and their ability to support each other through life's ups and downs. Retirement was just another phase in their journey, a chance to reflect on their careers, their friendships, and the legacy they wanted to leave behind.

As they sat in Sunset Park, overlooking the city they had called home for so long, they realized that retirement was not an end but a new beginning. With their humor and diversity as their guiding lights, they were ready to embrace this next chapter in life, cherishing each moment and making the most of their time together.

27. "The Wisdom of Age"

The years had flowed gracefully by, painting their lives with the brush of time. The eight friends who had forged an unbreakable bond in the hallowed halls of Sunset Park school were now in their late fifties. Though they had aged in body, their spirits remained as youthful and vibrant as ever.

Sunset Park in Brooklyn, with its memories etched into their souls, still served as their gathering place. The park had witnessed the ebb and flow of their lives, from youthful exuberance to the seasoned wisdom that comes with age. Their diverse backgrounds and unique senses of humor had been their constants throughout this journey.

Alex, still the same witty and sarcastic journalist of Greek descent, leaned back in his chair, peering at his lifelong friends. "You know, I've been thinking. We have aged like fine wine, my friends. Just with a few more wrinkles and perhaps a little less hair."

Lei, the Chinese-American tech wizard who had always excelled in his field but struggled with social interactions, could not help but smile. "Aging gracefully, Alex. And by the way, your hairline was receding even back in our twenties."

Rashida, the vivacious African-American actor celebrated for her vibrant slapstick comedy, chimed in with her trademark enthusiasm. "Truth be told, you've made up for that receding hairline with your sharp wit, Alex."

Carlos, the optimistic Puerto Rican musician who had faced career challenges in the turbulent world of music, chuckled. "Age hasn't dimmed your humor one bit, my friend."

Fatima, the Pakistani-American doctor who had navigated the delicate balance between family expectations and personal dreams, raised her glass in a toast. "Here's to growing older, wiser, and still managing to find the humor in life."

Elena, the Russian-Jewish lawyer known for her sharp tongue and heart of gold, added, "And to the enduring bonds that have kept us together through all these years."

Maya, the Afro-Latina artist who had delved into the depths of identity through her work, looked around at her friends, her eyes shimmering with warmth. "You know, as we've aged, we've also gained a deeper understanding of life and each other."

Their conversations had shifted over the years, from ambitious career aspirations and the joys of parenthood to discussions about retirement planning and the unique challenges of aging. Together, they had navigated the peaks and valleys of life, and these shared experiences had become a wellspring of wisdom and humor.

Lei, always the practical thinker, spoke up, his glasses perched on his nose. "Aging comes with its own set of challenges. We should start thinking about retirement planning, healthcare, and what we want our golden years to look like."

Rashida, the ever-creative spirit, could not help but chime in with her artistic flair. "And we can continue pursuing our passions, whether it's acting, music, or art. Age should never stop us from doing what we love."

Carlos nodded in fervent agreement. "I may not be the young musician I once was, but I can still create music and inspire others with my melodies."

Fatima, with her nurturing spirit, added, "Our health and well-being should be a priority. We can support each other in leading active and fulfilling lives, taking care of our bodies as we did our dreams."

Elena, with her sharp wit intact, could not resist a touch of humor. "And we can have regular debates about the state of the world, just like we used to. Age hasn't dulled our opinions, that's for sure."

Maya, always the insightful one, added, "Let's also use our accumulated wisdom to mentor the next generation, sharing our experiences and lessons with them. It's our way of giving back."

As they continued their discussions, they realized that aging was not just about the physical changes that came with it; it was also about embracing the richness of life's experiences. They had learned to find humor in the smallest moments, to cherish the moments they had, and to support each other through the challenges that came their way.

Their bond had deepened with age, and the wisdom they had gained was a testament to their enduring friendship. As they looked out at the familiar sights of Sunset Park, they knew that the joys and challenges of aging were just another chapter in their extraordinary journey together. With their humor and diversity, they were more than ready to face whatever life had in store for them in the years to come.

28. "Full Circle"

The hallowed halls of Sunset Park school had seen countless generations of students pass through its doors. It had been a witness to the laughter, the tears, and the dreams of children from diverse backgrounds. And now, as the golden years of their lives approached, the eight friends who had formed an unbreakable bond here found themselves back in the place where it had all begun.

Alex, ever the witty and sarcastic journalist of Greek descent, could not help but comment on the passage of time. "It feels like just yesterday that we were the ones starting kindergarten here."

Lei added, "Well, at least this time, none of us has to worry about being the new kid. We've got history here."

Rashida, the vivacious African-American actor, reminisced, "I remember how we used to put on impromptu plays during recess. Who would have thought some of us would end up in showbiz for real?"

Carlos, the optimistic Puerto Rican musician, chimed in, "And I used to play my guitar in the courtyard during lunch breaks. Those were simpler times."

Fatima, the Pakistani-American doctor, looked around at her friends and the new generation of parents bringing their children to school. "It's incredible how life comes full circle. We were once the ones starting school, and now we're here to see our own children and grandchildren off."

Elena, the Russian-Jewish lawyer with her sharp tongue and heart of gold, could not resist a bit of humor. "I have to say, our children are much more organized than we ever were. They've got schedules, color-coded folders, and a plan for everything."

Maya, the Afro-Latina artist who had delved into the depths of identity through her work, observed, "The diversity here is just as rich as it was when we were kids. It's heartwarming to see children from all walks of life coming together."

As they watched the new generation of children embark on their own educational journeys, they could not help but feel a sense of nostalgia. Sunset Park had shaped their lives in profound ways, instilling in them a deep appreciation for diversity, humor, and the enduring bonds of friendship.

They could not help but wonder what legacies they would leave behind for the next generation. Alex, always the reflective one, mused, "We've seen the world change in so many ways. We have faced challenges, celebrated victories, and cherished every moment together. What kind of legacy do we want to leave for these children?"

Lei, with her pragmatic outlook, replied, "We've learned the importance of friendship, diversity, and the ability to find humor in every situation. Perhaps those are the values we can pass on."

Rashida, the eternal optimist, added, "And we can inspire them to pursue their dreams, just as we did. Our journeys may have been different, but the spirit of perseverance is something we all share."

Carlos, always the dreamer, concluded, "Let's encourage them to embrace their passions, whatever they may be. Just as we found our paths, they'll find theirs."

As they stood in the place where their lifelong friendship had taken root, they realized that they had come full circle. They had started as children full of dreams and had grown into adults who had faced life's challenges with humor, diversity, and unwavering friendship.

Now, as they watched the new generation of children embark on their own adventures, they knew that Sunset Park would continue to be a place of growth, laughter, and dreams. And in the legacy, they left behind, the values of friendship, diversity, and the pursuit of dreams would forever endure.

Over the years, the bonds between these eight friends had only grown stronger. They had celebrated each other's successes, supported one another through hardships, and laughed through countless moments of joy and silliness. It was a friendship that had weathered the storms of life and had emerged even more resilient and enduring.

As they stood there, watching their children and grandchildren, they could not help but reflect on the lessons they had learned along the way. Alex, always the one with a sharp wit, quipped, "I suppose we're the wise elders now, dispensing wisdom and humor to the younger generation."

Lei, who had always struggled with social interactions, smiled warmly. "Yes, and maybe we can teach them that it's okay to be a little different, to embrace their quirks and unique qualities."

Rashida, with her vibrant personality, added, "And let's not forget the power of laughter. Life can throw some curveballs, but humor can help us through the toughest times."

Carlos nodded in agreement. "Absolutely, and they should never stop pursuing their dreams, no matter how big or small."

Fatima, the doctor who had balanced family expectations with her personal dreams, chimed in, "And let's remind them that they have a support system in us, just as we've had in each other."

Elena, with her sharp tongue and heart of gold, said, "And the importance of standing up for what's right, even when it's not the easiest path."

Maya, the artist who had explored her identity through her work, concluded, "And let's encourage them to express themselves, to find their own creative voices."

As the years had passed, their friendship had become a source of wisdom, guidance, and unwavering support for one another. They had shared the highs and lows of life, and now, they were ready to share their accumulated wisdom with the next generation.

It was a poignant moment, standing there in the schoolyard where their own stories had begun. They knew that their legacy would live on not only through their children and grandchildren but also through the values they had instilled in them—the values of friendship, diversity, humor, perseverance, and the pursuit of dreams.

As they watched the new generation of children laugh, play, and form their own friendships, they could not help but smile. The circle of life continued, and they were grateful to be a part of it, passing on the lessons they had learned and the love they had shared throughout the years.

In the end, it was not just about their own legacy; it was about the legacy of Sunset Park, a place where bonds were forged, dreams were nurtured, and friendships were cherished. And as they looked at each other, the laughter of children filling the air, they knew that their journey had come full circle, and the future was as bright as ever.

29. "Sunset Park Forever"

The streets of Sunset Park, Brooklyn, had witnessed the ebb and flow of life for generations. And as the sun dipped below the horizon, casting a warm, golden glow over the familiar neighborhood, the eight lifelong friends gathered one last time at the school that had been the epicenter of their shared history.

Alex, with his trademark wit and sarcasm, could not help but remark, "Well, here we are, back where it all began. Who would have thought we would meet up in the old neighborhood at this age?"

Lei, the tech whiz with her dry and unexpected humor, replied, "Life has a way of bringing us full circle. But hey, at least we can still work on a smartphone, right?"

Rashida, known for her vibrant slapstick comedy, chimed in, "And I can still do a mean pratfall, just like we used to in the schoolyard."

Carlos, the ever-optimistic musician who had faced career challenges, added, "Music might not have made me a superstar, but it's been the soundtrack of our lives."

Fatima, the doctor who had juggled family expectations with personal dreams, smiled warmly. "And we've all been there for each other through the highs and lows."

Elena, the sharp-tongued lawyer with a heart of gold, teased, "Even when I needed someone to bail me out of a sticky legal situation."

Maya, the artist who had explored her identity through her work, mused, "And I've painted every shade of Sunset Park in my art."

But there was an undeniable sense of nostalgia in the air. They had seen the world change, they had faced their own challenges, and they had celebrated their successes. Now, with retirement on the horizon, they had gathered one last time to relive the memories that had bound them together.

As they walked through the schoolyard, they could not help but reflect on the legacy they had built over the years. Sean, the

Irish-American firefighter who had always been the group's peacemaker, was no longer with them, but his spirit lived on in the laughter and camaraderie that filled the air.

They came across a group of children playing in the same courtyard where they had once played, and it brought tears to their eyes. The cycle of life continued, and they knew that their time here was drawing to a close.

Alex, always the reflective one, spoke up. "You know, we've learned a lot in our time here. About friendship, diversity, humor, perseverance, and the pursuit of dreams. These values have been the foundation of our lives."

Lei, pragmatic as ever, added, "And they'll continue to be our legacy, not just for us but for the generations that will come after us."

Rashida, with her eternal optimism, said, "Let's hope they find as much joy and laughter in their lives as we have in ours."

Carlos, the dreamer, concluded, "And let's remind them to keep chasing their dreams, no matter how old they get."

Fatima, with her unwavering support, chimed in, "And to have the courage to balance family expectations with personal dreams."

Elena, with a sly grin, teased, "And never forget the importance of standing up for what's right, even when it's not the easiest path."

Maya, the artist who had explored her identity through her work, concluded, "And to express themselves, to find their own creative voices, and to embrace their uniqueness."

They watched the children play, realizing that the legacy of Sunset Park would live on through the values they had instilled in the next generation. As the sun dipped below the horizon, casting long shadows across the schoolyard, they felt a profound sense of closure.

This final gathering in their beloved neighborhood was a testament to the enduring power of friendship, diversity, and humor. They had come full circle, and though the chapter of their lives in Sunset Park was coming to a close, the memories and values they had shared would forever endure.

As they stood there, hand in hand, watching the children run and laugh, they knew that Sunset Park had been more than just a place; it had been the backdrop to their lives, a place where they had formed unbreakable bonds and created lasting memories.

With one last glance around, they turned to each other, their faces reflecting the wisdom and joy of their years together. It was time to say goodbye to their beloved neighborhood, but the friendships they had forged would continue to flourish, no matter where life took them.

As they walked away from the schoolyard, their footsteps echoing in the fading light, they carried with them the spirit of Sunset Park, a spirit of friendship, diversity, and unwavering support. And as they looked ahead to the next chapter of their lives, they knew that the memories of their time here would forever be etched in their hearts.

Sunset Park had been their home, their sanctuary, and their source of inspiration. And as they embarked on new adventures and faced the unknown, they would always carry a piece of Sunset Park with them, a reminder of the enduring bonds of friendship and the values that had shaped their lives.

As they walked away from their final gathering, they knew that Sunset Park would forever hold a special place in their hearts. The neighborhood had given them a lifetime of memories, and those memories would be their cherished treasure, a reminder of the laughter, the tears, and the love they had shared.

With a bittersweet smile, they whispered their farewells to Sunset Park, knowing that the legacy of their friendship would live on, not just in the neighborhood, but in their hearts and in the hearts of the generations they had touched.

And as they walked into the future, hand in hand, they carried with them the lessons, the laughter, and the love of a lifetime spent in Sunset Park. For this final gathering was not an end, but a new beginning, a testament to the enduring power of friendship and the bonds that would forever hold them together.

Sunset Park had been their home, their sanctuary, and their source of inspiration. And as they embarked on new adventures and faced the unknown, they would always carry a piece of Sunset Park with them, a reminder of the enduring bonds of friendship and the values that had shaped their lives.

30. "The Last Sunset"

As the golden sun dipped below the horizon, casting a warm, amber glow over the familiar streets of Sunset Park, the eight friends (Sean's spirit still with them) for life gathered one last time. The school where their journey had begun, where they had laughed, cried, and forged bonds stronger than time itself, stood as a silent witness to their reunion. Ten years had passed since Sean, the Irish-American firefighter, had unexpectedly left this world, and life had continued its inexorable march.

Alex, with a penchant for political satire, arrived first. His gray-streaked hair and a few extra wrinkles around his eyes were evidence of the passage of time, but his sharp humor remained as incisive as ever. He looked around at the schoolyard, a nostalgic smile playing on his lips. "Seems like just yesterday we were causing trouble in this place."

Lei, the tech-savvy Chinese-American, arrived next. Her dry and unexpected humor was still intact, and she held her smartphone with a look of perpetual confusion, as if it were a perplexing alien artifact. "Well, at least I finally figured out how to use emojis properly," she quipped, her eyes twinkling.

Rashida, the African-American aspiring actor known for her vibrant slapstick comedy, arrived in a burst of laughter. Her infectious joy and magnetic energy had not dimmed one bit. "Darlings, you won't believe the auditions I've been to lately! I'm still the queen of pratfalls."

Carlos, the optimistic and naive Puerto Rican musician who had faced his share of career challenges, arrived with his guitar slung over his shoulder. "I may not have become a rock star, but I still make music every day. That is what counts, right?"

Fatima, the Pakistani-American doctor balancing family expectations with personal dreams, strolled in, her serene smile belying the challenges she had overcome. "I've delivered so many babies, saved lives, and still managed to paint in my spare time."

Elena, the sharp-tongued Russian-Jewish lawyer with a heart of gold, could not resist a sarcastic remark. "I've defended countless clients, won cases, and alienated a few judges along the way. Some things never change."

Maya, the Afro-Latina artist who had explored her identity through her work, arrived with a sketchbook in hand. "My art has evolved, but my passion for self-expression remains the same."

As they exchanged stories and laughter, they felt a profound sense of gratitude for the enduring friendships that had shaped their lives. Sunset Park had been their anchor, the place where they had discovered themselves and each other. But they knew it was time to say goodbye.

The group decided to take a stroll through the neighborhood one last time. They passed by the corner store where they had bought their favorite snacks as kids, the park where they had played countless games, and the diner where they had shared late-night meals.

Their steps eventually led them to the school rooftop, where they had spent countless afternoons watching the sunset and dreaming of the future. As they gazed at the now-familiar skyline of New York City, a sense of closure and contentment washed over them.

"We've come a long way, haven't we?" Alex mused; his gaze fixed on the horizon.

Lei nodded; her eyes misty. "But we've always had each other."

Rashida, ever the optimist, chimed in, "And we'll always have the memories."

Carlos strummed a few chords on his guitar, and the others joined in with a bittersweet melody, a tribute to the bonds that had sustained them through the years.

As the sun sank below the cityscape, painting the sky in hues of orange and purple, they stood together, a testament to the enduring power of friendship. In that moment, they knew that no matter where life took them, the spirit of Sunset Park would forever be a part of their souls.

With arms linked and hearts full, they descended from the rooftop, ready to face the next chapter of their lives with the wisdom of age, the hope of the future, and the laughter of friends who had become family.

And so, as the last rays of the sun disappeared, they walked away from their beloved neighborhood, their heads held high, and their spirits lifted by the knowledge that the bonds they had forged would endure, just like the sunset over Sunset Park.

The End.

~ ~ ~ ~ ~

Epilogue:

The sun dipped below the horizon, casting a warm, golden glow over the familiar streets of Sunset Park. The same streets that had witnessed the laughter, tears, and countless shared moments of a group of friends who had become more like family.

As the years passed, the eight friends for life had weathered every storm and celebrated every triumph. They had grown together, evolved, and seen the world change around them. Yet, one thing remained constant—their unwavering bond.

In the twilight of their lives, they gathered once more in their beloved neighborhood, reminiscing about the journey that had brought them to this moment. Lines etched with time adorned their faces, but their eyes still sparkled with the same humor, diversity, and enduring friendship that had defined them from the beginning.

The legacy they had created was not one of fame or fortune, but of love, resilience, and the profound impact of human connection. They had faced life's challenges head-on, offering each other unwavering support, and had celebrated life's joys with unbridled enthusiasm.

As the last rays of sunlight bathed Sunset Park, they raised their glasses to the memories they had made, the laughter they had shared, and the unbreakable bonds that had sustained them through the years. Their stories, etched into the very soul of their neighborhood, would live on as a testament to the enduring spirit of friendship.

With a sense of fulfillment, they looked ahead to the future, knowing that the legacy they had created would continue to inspire generations to come. In their hearts, Sunset Park would forever remain a place of love, laughter, and the timeless bonds of friendship.

And so, as the sun set on their final gathering, they walked away hand in hand, their laughter echoing through the streets, leaving behind a legacy of love that would endure for all time—a testament to the enduring power of the human spirit and the remarkable journey of the friends for life.

~ ~ ~ ~ ~

Dedication

To the enduring spirit of friendship,

This tale is dedicated to those who understand the profound impact of laughter, diversity, and the bonds of friendship. To the friends who have become family, and the family who have become friends, this story is for you.

May the Sunset Park Chronicles serve as a reminder that in the tapestry of life, it is the threads of love, humor, and shared moments that weave the most beautiful patterns. Through the ups and downs, the laughter, and tears, you have shown that friendship is a treasure beyond measure.

In the pages that you read find reflections of your own enduring bonds and the belief that, no matter where life may lead, the timeless connection of true friendship will always guide the way.

With deepest gratitude for the warmth and humor you bring to the world,

Always grateful,
Kevin James Joseph McNamara

~ ~

#KevinJamesJosephMcNamara
#KevinJJosephMcNamara
#KevinJJMcNamara

The Sunset Park Chronicles
A Journey of Laughter, Friendship, and Endless Memories